ISBN Electronic Version: 978-0-9925415-0-7
ISBN Print Version: 978-0-9925415-1-4

THE EYE OF SHIVA

SAM TAYLOR

4

The Eye of Shiva

Shiva Kiran and Zokar Rizian are living in a changed galaxy. The Galactic Union is rebuilding its fleet, led by a furious Empress hell-bent on avenging the destruction of her battle fleet by the humans. Earth and the Fey alliance are battling for existence on the edge of a galactic empire which wants them obliterated. But old alliances within the empire come back to haunt Zokar Rizian, and he finds himself on the outer with his captain.

Shiva, for his part, is puzzled by his own complete lack of psychic ability. His is the purest human blood of all, so why should he be unlike the rest of the powerful humans around him? But then the tides of war turn against them, and all such considerations must be put on hold.

Prologue

The little Grey alien was thin, almost starving. He had not eaten for weeks, and had reached the stage of desperation where he was only just strong enough to hunt. He was reckless. His oversized black eyes were slightly dull and hazy, his skin and suckers paper-dry. His mind was on food; food for the mind.

His tiny escape pod had landed, roughly, several kilometres inside Yosemite National Park, and he had seen no life forms in the steep terrain. But now he heard a voice, a strange alien patter which galvanized his whole body into pursuit. He came up behind the lone human female at a shambling gallop, then launched his skinny, metre-tall form at the human's head, reaching out with the suckers on his fingers to grasp the psi-points on the face, ears and neck. The human tried to scream as she fell, but only got out a single harsh cry before the alien's sucker-like body wrapped itself around her face, blocking her mouth and nose. The phone she had been talking into clattered on to the rocks by the path. The human made muffled screaming noises, reaching up and pulling ineffectually at the Grey with panicked hands, but the alien did not notice. The human instinctively put out her protective white aura, but that only hastened the process of feeding as the aura was absorbed directly into the alien's skin. They writhed in the dust of the trail, but he did not feel the rough sand and rocks scratching his body. He felt only one thing…. the intake of energy.

His starving mind was drinking in the rich harvest of thoughts, the unexpectedly strong telepathic emanations of the human's mind pouring into his psyche like a warm balm.

He could not have stopped if he had tried, as his mind sucked the thoughts out of the human's head. He surrendered himself to the ecstasy of quenching the overwhelming thirst in his mind, and slowly the struggles of the human ceased.

Many minutes later, he sat up and stared at the human, poking at her with a toe. He stroked the human's hair and said something to her. He frowned and looked glum when there was no response, then staggered off looking for water. Guilt overwhelmed him as he realized that he had taken a life. Only the long starvation that he had suffered, on the trip to Earth through the Void, had brought him to the point of desperation which had led to his uncontrolled attack on the hapless human. Tears of shame began to roll down from the big dark eyes of the alien as he limped along the path.

Chapter One

Zokar Rizian and his captain, Shiva Kiran, emerged from the back of a small, quiet pub on Earth without attracting too much attention, their stomachs full of rum and steak. They walked in companionable silence over to an air car and climbed in the front. From the back seat two massive, sleek, feline heads lifted up sleepily. Zokar took the air car up and headed for a nearby supermarket, setting his mouth in a grimmer line than usual at the thought of the attention they would attract from the naturally curious Terrans at the shopping centre. Zokar knew that his pointed ears, silver eyes and six foot eight height attracted attention wherever he went on Earth, but Shiva, although entirely human, was still a handsome six foot four blond with blue eyes, and attracted his fair share of attention. Zokar glanced at Shiva a couple of times and asked, "Have you enjoyed your stay on Earth?"

Shiva started a little, and Zokar realized he must have been half asleep. Shiva grinned sheepishly and said, "Now that I've had a decent meal."

Zokar smiled, "Only a human could starve on a planet with such an abundance of raw fish."

"Ugh," smiled Shiva, "Whose idea was it to go camping anyway? Only an elf could live on sushi and fresh air."

Zokar smiled, but said nothing as he piloted the car down towards the shopping centre. As they approached the humans below he automatically became aware of the reassuring weight of his blasters hugging the inside of his wrists. Not, he mused, that they would do him any real good against Terran humans.

What neither Zokar nor Shiva saw as the car descended was a Grey alien duck back under the eaves of the shopping centre as the air car approached. The Grey wriggled its way back into the ceiling space of the centre, where dozens of its kind sheltered. The Greys all stayed very still as the air car hummed down past the roof. They looked sidelong at each other with their huge dark eyes in the dim light coming from under the eaves.

In the back of the car, Gan, the black cat, growled in his throat, earning a quizzical glance from Shiva. Ghrian, the golden cat with the blue eyes, sniffed the air suspiciously.

Zokar dropped the car down onto the tarmac of the parking lot, and the big cats leapt gracefully out onto the ground. Nearby, a woman in a yellow dress and high heels was putting bags of shopping into an air car boot. Unlike their open car, hers was a closed-in model. Zokar ignored her and walked on, with Shiva. He turned to check the cats, and saw them yawning and stretching behind him. As he walked past the woman, however, he heard the whirr of a car window opening, then a cry from the woman of "No! Simba!"

Zokar turned to see a tiny dog no bigger than his hand leap out of the woman's air car and make straight for the big cats, yapping furiously. Gan sniffed curiously at the tiny yapping creature, but immediately the tiny dog ran forward and bit his nose. Gan roared deafeningly and swatted at it, pinning it under a paw. The woman screamed and grabbed the dog's trailing leash, and Shiva yelled, "Gan! No!" The dog twisted around and bit Gan's paw and Gan yelped and lifted his paw. The tiny dog shot out, but then ran straight into the mouth of the other cat Ghrian, who closed his mouth with a snap. Zokar began to laugh.

The woman let out a howl of horror, and Shiva roared, 'spit it out!" to Ghrian, who glared at him, then went cross-eyed as the little dog began to yap inside his cavernous mouth. Zokar was still unable to do anything but laugh, but suddenly he felt a solid blow against his chest and realized that the woman had hit him with a shopping bag. Zokar felt his face tighten in anger and pulled out his disruptor, but Shiva shoved his hand upwards just as Zokar pulled the trigger, so the shot went just over her head. Shiva cried, "No! Zokar!"

"What? She wouldn't shut up, and she hit me!" protested Zokar angrily. The woman had dropped the leash and was standing there hyperventilating, for the blast of the laser had shot through her hair. It had missed her scalp by only millimetres, leaving a tunnel of fried hair through her elaborate hairstyle.

The black cat, Gan, slyly took the forgotten end of the leash and began to chew along it thoughtfully as Shiva and Zokar argued.

"How else was I supposed to shut her up?" demanded Zokar, glaring at the woman.

"You can't just go shooting people!" chided Shiva, "And Ghrian, spit that out!"

Ghrian looked sulky but spat out a mouthful of sodden, slimy dog. It looked even smaller than it had when dry. It promptly began to growl at the two big cats again. It tried to run back to the woman, but found its leash held by Gan's teeth. Gan looked at it evilly and kept chewing along the leash. The dog began to yodel in distress as it felt itself dragged slowly towards Gan's teeth. It spread out its legs like sticks and put out its claws, scratching desperate lines across the pavement.

Shiva stepped up to Gan, tugged the leash from his mouth with a jerk and handed the sodden end to the woman. She stared at them, then placed her soggy little dog back in the car and closed the door. Then she just sat there, shaking and staring out the front. The little dog shook itself furiously, sending a shower of cat saliva all over its owner, the upholstery and the inside of the windows.

"I can't take you lot anywhere!" exclaimed Shiva. He

glared at Zokar and the two cats and started walking across the large car park towards the shop.

Something dawned suddenly on Zokar and he asked, "Why didn't she stop us?"

"What?" Shiva's voice was snappy.

"She's a Terran. Why didn't she just use her psychic powers and stop us?"

"I don't know. Shock maybe? Zokar, you have to stop blasting people whenever they annoy you."

"Why? What do you want me to do, hug them?" asked Zokar sarcastically.

Shiva looked up at him then hesitated. "Maybe we'd better leave these two in the car," he sighed, and turned back. Zokar shook his head, but turned to follow him.

They returned to the air car and put the cats back in, telling them sternly to stay. Zokar watched the woman with the dog drive jerkily away, hitting a signpost on the way but not stopping. He smiled and followed Shiva across the car park and into the store.

Immediately they noticed raised voices coming from up near the shop counter. Zokar, who had been about to head eagerly for the well-stocked meat shelves, hesitated, taking in the scenario playing out at the counter.

"Never a dull moment," Shiva murmured with a faint smile. Zokar scowled, but felt his interest growing.

"I love Earth," muttered Zokar. "They're always doing something interesting here."

The counter was deep within the shop. A young man was pressed aggressively against it, screaming abuse at the proprietor and waving a gun inches in front of his face. The proprietor, a tall, middle aged man with dark brown hair and glasses, was shaking with suppressed fury but taking money out of the till and stuffing it in a canvas bank bag.

Zokar shot a meaningful glance at Shiva, then scanned the rest of the shop with his eyes. The elf tilted his head and raised a silver eyebrow at the front counter, then asked Shiva, "Why does that human not have his protective aura up by now?"

Shiva shook his head, and whispered quietly back, "Nor do the intruders."

"What should we do?" asked Zokar.

"Help, of course," said Shiva, shooting Zokar an exasperated look.

"Help the robbers?" asked Zokar hopefully, visions of shelves full of free pre-packaged fish filling his head.

"No... sheesh, Zokar, we help the shopkeeper!" hissed Shiva back.

"Because he owns more things?" guessed Zokar.

Shiva was still shaking his head, "Because it's the right thing to do."

Zokar felt disappointed and puzzled, but shrugged his acquiescence. Shiva was, after all, his captain.

Shiva nodded his head at the shelves behind them and walked up to the counter behind the robber.

Zokar scouted out the rest of the store and found another occupant, a twitchy young man with a drawn knife and a hooded jacket, who turned with a glare to Zokar, but shrank slightly into himself when he had to look up to the elf's six-foot-eight height. He took in Zokar's cold silver eyes and alien appearance and shuffled slightly away from Zokar, looking suddenly nervous. Zokar did nothing, just lifted an item off the shelf and stared at it as though considering buying it. His eyes were on Shiva up at the counter. His finely pointed elvish ears, however, pressed back around his skull, tracking every movement of the human behind him.

What no one saw were two tail tips swishing along behind the shelves inside the front of the store. Gan and Ghrian had heard the raised voices, left the air car and snuck into the store, ducking low to avoid the automatic door chime. The big cats had been aggravated by the incident with the small dog, and they did not like strangers who raised their voices, especially not around Shiva and Zokar.

The man with the gun up at the front counter was still

yelling, but he stopped when Shiva asked mildly over the noise, "Hello. May I please have two hot coffees?"

The clerk goggled at him, and the robber spun around and yelled, "What the hell do you think you're doing?" He waved his gun at Shiva. Further down the store, Zokar noticed this and frowned.

"Getting coffees," Zokar heard Shiva say mildly.

Zokar smiled at a shuffling noise behind him as the young man in the hood braced to move. He lunged at Zokar from behind, but Zokar did not move his feet, merely disposed of the threat with a backwards snap of his elbow. Zokar screwed up his mouth ruefully as he heard the sickening snap of a human neck as the young man slumped to the floor behind him. He had only meant to incapacitate the man, but he kept forgetting how short humans were. It was so easy to deliver a sharp blow intended for the solar plexus, only to find he had snapped their necks instead. Shiva would be angry with him again. Zokar did not bother looking back at the fallen accomplice though, but kept his attention on what was happening at the front counter.

The robber at the counter said to Shiva, in an enraged falsetto, "Fuck, man, I'm robbing this place. Mind if I finish what I'm doing, first?"

"Oh, go ahead, don't let me stop you," smiled Shiva mildly. Zokar strolled silently up towards Shiva.

The robber stared amazed at Shiva, then turned. His wild eyes locked with Zokar's for a moment and widened. He glanced down and behind Zokar, who realised he must have seen the body on the floor behind him. The elf tensed, but then relaxed when he saw Shiva's hand move towards the disruptor on his belt. But then Zokar heard a strange scuffling behind him and spun around, his disruptor slipping forward into his hand before he had finished the turn. Zokar swore as he saw Gan's great black claws reach out from under the shelves and tug the body of the dead robber further back into the store. Zokar heard a gasp and turned back just in time to see the other robber's finger tightening on the trigger of the gun in his hand. The gun was aimed squarely at Zokar's chest, and Zokar realised he could not fire back because Shiva would be caught in the halo of his disruptor.

Zokar leapt aside, but the gun did not fire. Instead there was the sudden whistle of a disruptor, and the robber's head exploded into a thousand pieces, splattering the shelves and merchandise with a spray of red blood.

"That's not nice," Zokar heard Shiva say mildly. Zokar turned his head just in time to see Shiva holster his still-glowing disruptor. The headless corpse stood motionless before Shiva for several seconds, the convulsive tightening of all the body's muscles freezing it momentarily in a standing position, before gravity took over and it toppled to the floor.

Zokar inclined his head to Shiva, "Thank you." They stood there looking down at the decapitated body. "But tell me, why is it alright for you to blast humans, but not for me?"

Shiva just chuckled and pointed at the body twitching at his feet, "Because that's a *bad* human."

Zokar frowned, "I see."

Shiva smiled up at him, "No, you don't."

Zokar sighed and said, "No. But sometimes I think you make up these 'ethics' you tell me about."

Shiva turned away with a shrug and a slow wink at Zokar.

Feline eyes peered out from under the first shopping aisle.

Shiva smiled and said politely to the clerk, who was pressed in amongst the drink machines with a face as white as a sheet, "I'm very sorry about the mess. May we have our coffees now, please?"

The clerk's head nodded obediently, although his mouth opened and shut like a fish's for a few moments before he managed to reply, indicating the coffee machine to their left, "On the house."

Shiva and Zokar looked at him blankly.

The clerk managed to find his voice again and explained, "It's free."

"Oh, thanks!" said Shiva, and walked over to fiddle with the machine for a few moments. There was a clunk and a hiss, and Shiva handed the elf a coffee, "Here you go, Zokar."

The clerk, who had been dubiously inspecting the two bodies of the robbers and the mess at the front of his store, looked up with interest when Shiva said Zokar's name.

Zokar smiled and took the coffee, "Amazing. You can't read any of the Terran languages, but you can get coffee from anything within ten seconds."

The clerk asked, "Zokar? Not Zokar Rizian?"

Shiva and Zokar looked at each other, then back at the clerk, and Zokar nodded warily, feeling his hand close around his disruptor, "Yes?"

"Oh, man, it's a pleasure. Hey, you want anything else in the store, you just take it, eh?"

"Anything?" Zokar was pleased, and relaxed his grip on his gun. The clerk nodded, and Zokar looked around him, then picked up the empty cash register, pulling it loose from its mooring cables with a gentle tug. Shiva looked at him curiously as the steel cables snapped in rapid succession.

"I've always wanted one of these," shrugged Zokar, tucking it under one arm. Shiva sighed, but looked interested when he saw a potato chip stand.

A few minutes later, the clerk watched them leave with their coffees, the cash register, and quite a few packets of potato chips. Then he choked back a scream as what looked like an oversized golden lion, with unnaturally blue eyes, cleared the first row of shelves, snatched up the headless body of the robber as though it were a rag doll, and trotted out behind Shiva and Zokar. The clerk could not move and simply stared numbly as an equally huge creature that looked like a black panther trotted out with the body of the second robber.

Gan and Ghrian were a little exasperated with their masters. The human and the elf had made kills, yet were leaving the spoils behind. Gan shook his head slightly, sighing around his awkward mouthful of dead human. Trust their masters to forget the carcases: they were so like kittens, sometimes. It was just as well they had the two grown-up cats with them to look after them.

Zokar and Shiva were only a few metres out into the car park when they heard the sound of approaching sirens. Four police cars screamed to a halt around them and soon gun muzzles surrounded Shiva and Zokar. Zokar felt a Shiva put a restraining hand on his arm and glared at the police but did nothing. The clerk ran out, and said, "No, no, it wasn't them, you don't understand," but then he stopped at the sight of the two great cats holding the corpses of the robbers.

Shiva turned around and snapped, "I thought I told you two to stay in the car? And what have I said about eating humans?" The cats hung their heads guiltily, but without dropping the robbers' bodies.

Zokar said out of the corner of his mouth, without taking his silver eyes off the police, "Shiva, I don't think this looks terribly good."

Zokar watched Shiva look down at the armful of potato chips he was carrying, then over at the cash register under Zokar's arm, then back at the two big cats carrying a still-dripping corpse each.

The senior sergeant in front of them glowered up at them and said tightly, "You're damned right it doesn't, sonny."

It took quite a bit of explaining from the store clerk, but eventually the police allowed Shiva and Zokar to leave, Zokar clutching his cash register happily. As they walked back towards their air car, two body bags floated past them on gurneys into a waiting ambulance. The cats watched the bodies pass with glaring eyes.

They stole our masters' kills, thought Gan, and Ghrian met his eyes. The two big cats looked around thoughtfully. The police had all gone back into the store and left their air cars powered down and sitting on the tarmac with the cabins exposed. Gan and Ghrian casually wended their way in between the police cars, hesitating briefly by each police vehicle as they made their way back to their own air car.

"Hurry up, you two!" called Shiva impatiently. The two big cats gambolled back and leapt into the air car, earning them raised eyebrows from Zokar and Shiva as the car wobbled in response to the cats' combined weight. Zokar powered the car up and banked steeply up into the air.

As the car rose up past the roof space of the shopping centre, the two cats flattened their ears and swished their tails, sniffing the air warily. Far below them, a Grey alien emerged after the air car had risen up above the roof, and slunk around to the end of the roof top, staring after the air car curiously.

Back at the store, a policeman came back to his car, then stopped and stared at the smoking, dissolved mess that was his upholstery. He leaned forward and sniffed at the smoke, then squinted his eyes shut and pulled a face at the stench. His sergeant came out and demanded, "What's the hold-up?"

The young officer turned to his sergeant, his face screwed up, "What's that smell?"

The sergeant sniffed, then looked at him incredulously, "Is that *cat piss*?"

Chapter Two

Tom paced restlessly in the vast enclosure. The floor was flat, polished grey. The walls and ceiling were a lighter grey. The windows showed complete blackness, except for the occasional star ship sliding across the blackness then disappearing, and a few tiny, vague clouds of light in the distance; distant galaxies. Tom waited patiently in the queue as two elves got themselves coffee, then shuffled up to the outlet and pressed the button. A cup materialised instantly, full of lukewarm, black coffee. Tom curled his lips at the bitter taste of the sugarless coffee, but walked away with it anyway; it was all he would get.

He did not feel like playing chess or computer games. He automatically turned to look as a brief argument broke out between an elvish inmate and a tall, pugnacious looking human. Tom debated stepping in, but the two turned their backs on each other and walked away. He couldn't blame them for being irritable and bored. He sighed and sat on one of the many hard bench spaces around the walls, looking down at his huge, brown hands wrapped around the coffee cup.

Tom's mind wandered back to the night in the hospital when he had awoken with a fright to see the liquid black eyes of a grey alien looming over him in the night. He had stared at the alien through a haze of pain, and then, to his amazement, felt the pain begin to ebb away slowly. The alien had said something in that strange, drawn out language of theirs, and bent over Tom with a strange buzzing device. Tom had awoken here, and had been here ever since. His health had returned rapidly, and he waited patiently to find out what the greys wanted with him.

It took a long time, but Tom came eventually to the sad conclusion that the greys didn't need anything from him but his thoughts; or rather, the energy from his thoughts. Thought energy to a Grey was like food to a human. It sustained them. Rather than physically hunt or harvest their own food, the Greys tapped directly into the already-processed energy of the human mind and spirit.

The Greys held about a hundred prisoners: men, women and Fey mostly, with only a couple of elves. The elves weren't any use to the Greys, being practically psi-null and thus not a good food source. This put the elves always a little on edge, thinking that at any moment they might be pushed out an airlock rather than fed and cared for. It was what elves would have done with redundant inmates, and the elves could not understand why the Greys did not do it to them.

Outside the airlock was nothing but the deep blackness of the place they called the Void; in this case the space between the galaxy containing Earth and its neighbouring galaxy, Andromeda. The station was so far out in the Void, that if two ships left Earth at the same time, and one turned for the galaxy's core, and the other headed for Andromeda, the first ship could travel to the galaxy's core and back to Earth again, before the second ship reached the space station.

Their captors were the aliens known on Earth as common Grey aliens; hairless, innocuous looking little creatures with skinny limbs. Their huge black ovoid eyes were set in similarly ovoid heads with tiny mouths and near invisible nostrils. They were about a metre tall and their skin was pale grey all over. Their voices sounded like someone trying unsuccessfully to tune a violin; almost human, but drawn out and distorted.

Tom watched one of the captives, a small Fey woman with the silver hair and eyes of her kind, tug at her solid metal collar, which was about five centimetres wide, and about two centimetres deep with rounded edges. It had the soft, pure sheen of gold. All the prisoners wore them. Several of the prisoners also wore bracelets of the same gold.

Tom wore a full gold helmet continuous with his collar, with an opening in the front to show his face. Dark curls escaped below the helmet, and his body was powerful, with brown skin and huge hands. He wandered over to the Fey woman, put a hand on her shoulder, and said quietly, "How are you going, M'rinda?"

She turned her triangular, pale face up to him and regarded him with silver eyes and smiled, "Hey, Tom, not too bad, I just-"

Just then however, there were noises in the corridor outside their enclosure. Most of the prisoners jumped up and ran back to the walls, pressing themselves as far as they could back into the cold steel. Tom moved too, but rather than running, strolled over casually behind M'rinda.

To the collective relief of the prisoners, the guards were delivering a prisoner, not taking one out. M'rinda gasped as the guards flung a figure to the floor inside the doorway. The body landed with a loud clang and a clatter. His head was encased in a similar gold helmet to Tom's and his body was covered with long robes.

The guards left and the crumpled figure on the floor was deathly still. The small crowd of prisoners eventually approached warily, but the figure on the floor did not stir. M'rinda crouched down and touched him, trying to lever him over onto his back, and gasped. The helmet covered his whole face, with only tiny holes for his eyes, nose and mouth. She tutted in sympathy, and called, "Tom, come and see." Tom came over and pulled at the prone figure's arm and he and M'rinda both gasped.

The creature on the floor had dark robes and clothes on, made of quite beautiful, rich fabric. But under that fabric, on every limb and all around his torso, he was encased in a suit of gold. It was intricately crafted, jointed at all the man's joints and conforming to his body shape, but the gold was so thick that Tom thought that the suit in total must weigh over four hundred kilograms.

"Here, give me a hand, we can't leave him like this. Help me lift him onto one of those sofas," said Tom to the other prisoners around him.

It took ten men to lift him off the floor and place him carefully on one of the low couches at the edge of the room. He lay there unconscious for many hours, the other occupants of the prison giving him a wide berth but watching him anxiously for any signs of life.

Chapter Three

Trudi Saint James shook her head, her dark hair shimmering as it swayed with the movement. Beside her, a hulking Earth man peered into the view screen she was surveying, "Is that Zokar and Captain Shiva?" he asked, looking at the circle of police cars with two tall men in the centre of a circle of guns. The scene on the screen changed to show a woman in a yellow dress yelling something at the reporter, then holding up a slimy-looking little creature that looked like a cross between a large rat and a very wet dog.

"Send a shuttle down there and pick them up," sighed Trudi. "And then have the shuttle meet me and Laura at Coastal Bunker Five."

"You mean the Palace," he grinned.

"It's a bunker."

Nick shrugged, grinned and said, "Aye aye, Ma'am."

About ten miles from Coastal Bunker Five, Laura Saint James awoke to the sound of distant, excited whinnies from her horse. The tall mare was tied to a low tree just back from the shore. Laura sat up, and realised that the tide had come in, and there was a much wider stretch of water between the headland where she had fallen asleep and the shore. Whereas before only about every tenth or fifteenth wave had lightly splashed the top of the rock where she lay, now every wave sent a firm splash of cool salt water onto her. The mare in the distance was circling restlessly back and forth around the tree to which Laura had tied her at low tide. Laura sighed, and lowered herself back into the now chilly water. Something brushed against her leg. It was probably the rocks, she decided, then as she swam out away from the rocks she saw it: a triangular fin cutting the water, over a half a metre high.

Laura breathed a sigh of relief, concentrated, and felt for the simple mind of the predator with her thoughts. Slowly the fin turned and moved over to her, and she grasped the front of it with her hand gently but firmly. The Great White obediently turned and swam strongly towards the beach, then when Laura was about ten metres out from shore, she released the creature's fin. The shark turned on its side, the huge eye surveying her, then it turned and disappeared under the waves. Laura swam the few metres left to shore. The shark had saved her a good hour's swim against the already strongly ebbing tide, for which she was grateful. She still had an hour's ride home.

The mare had frozen and stared at her in response to her arrival, perhaps sensing the shark. But now the horse spun around and looked intently off in the direction of the palace. From this far along the beach, the mist from the waves made the palace a distant, white mirage. Laura looked along the beach as she walked up the beach to the mare, and saw three horses in the distance, galloping along the beach towards her. As Laura arrived next to the mare, the horse whinnied loudly. Laura flinched at the loud noise, but was busy concentrating on the approaching riders.

The lead rider suddenly leapt up to stand on the saddle of his powerful white horse, holding the reins down at his hip, laughing at the fun of it all.

"Shiva," smiled Laura, watching him admiringly. His riding skills had developed rapidly over the last few months, and so had Zokar's, under the stern tutelage of Trudi.

Behind him Zokar, not to be outdone, leaned forward then jumped to his feet on his saddle with the easy agility of his kind. Behind them both galloped Trudi, who stayed sensibly seated in her saddle. The group of horses thundered up the beach towards her. The mare tied next to Laura reared up with excitement, snapping her tie rope and galloping out to join the other horses.

"Damn!" exclaimed Laura, watching her mare circle the other horses then leave them and gallop full-pelt back along the endless white sand towards the palace.

Shiva rode up and leapt from his standing position straight down to the sand, still running, kicking up long arcs of sand with each foot. He swept her up in his arms, said, "Hey, beautiful!" and kissed her enthusiastically.

"Oi!" Laura shrieked, "You're all sandy!"

"Oh, yeah, we stopped for a swim earlier," grinned Shiva, watching her spit sand from her mouth. He turned to look at her mare, which was now a distant dot on the beach, "Want a lift home?"

"Well, yes, please, since you have frightened my horse off," she smiled, delighted to see him.

Zokar and Trudi rode up, both smiling broadly at Laura.

"Hi, Zokar, Tru," smiled Laura.

"Hey, sis!" smiled Trudi.

"You let your animal go?" asked Zokar, puzzled.

Shiva leapt back up onto the white horse's back.

Trudi grinned, "Smart girl. Now she gets to ride double with Shiva."

"Oh, I see," said Zokar. He waited until both Trudi and Laura's backs were turned, reached for his disruptor and aimed it at Trudi's horse, but Shiva caught his eye and shook his head vigorously. Zokar shrugged, sighed and holstered his disruptor.

"I might live longer if I don't ride with you," said Laura, looking dubiously at Shiva's hand being offered to her from atop his horse, which was still plunging up and down with excitement. Hesitantly she accepted his hand, and felt herself whisked easily up in front of Shiva, into his bronzed arms. He smiled, pulled her close and turned his horse's head for home and squeezed his bare legs into its side, holding the reins around Laura. The horse, still excited as it was, returned readily to a gallop, and Laura found herself in the precarious position of racing breakneck across the sand sitting well forward of her usual riding position, with only his arms to hold her. Shiva's arms were firm about her, though, and eventually she relaxed.

After a while her mind drifted and she remembered the last time someone had doubled her on a horse like this. It was M'rel, the Fey girl who had first found Laura stuck on Earth. *M'rel*, though Laura sadly, missing her a little. M'rel could ride like the wind, and fly a spaceship like you wouldn't believe. *Well, she used to be able to, before I killed her*, thought Laura… *her, my brother and a hundred and twenty thousand other people.* Shiva felt her shudder against him and tightened his hold around her reassuringly, "Don't worry, you won't fall."

"I already have," she whispered, but her words were lost in the pounding of hooves, the roaring of waves and the whistling of the wind past their ears. She thought of Dom, and her mind instinctively reached out for the twin bond, but found nothing but blackness and emptiness.

Chapter Four

The man on the Grey alien base deep in the void came back to consciousness slowly, and felt his dark hair matted with perspiration around his strong face. He blinked, and sighed. For once the headache that plagued him was gone. He tried to move his powerful limbs, but felt restraints, and groaned. To his relief, apart from the restraints, the gold suit seemed to have gone. His current situation was a result of yet another failed escape attempt. He stared around him at the huge machines which were linked into wires, which spread out into a spray of electrodes affixed to his head. He groaned, sensing that the machinery was draining his mind just as the Greys did, and keeping him helpless in his restraints. He listened carefully and realized the machinery was gradually slowing in tempo.

He turned his head and saw the familiar dark grey face of the chief guard.

"You haf awoken," said the guard, his large oval head with its massive, liquid, almond-shaped eyes fixed on the man's face. He stood to approach the bench where the man was bound.

"My arms hurt," said the dark haired man. His midnight blue eyes followed the alien.

"That is unfortunate. I am afraid you are too dangerous to release, even for a short time," murmured the guard, coming up and putting a cold hand sympathetically on the man's arm. The man snatched it away as well as he could, making the restraints clink, and glared at the alien.

"One day, I will get free. Maybe not today, nor tomorrow.... but one day," and his tone of voice and expression indicated that would not be a good day for his jailer.

The alien shrugged, "Possibly. It is my concern to ensure that does not happen, my Lord."

"How long have I been here?" the man asked.

"Long enough for you to recover your strength. Time for uss to eat," sighed the alien.

The man groaned, as his headache returned, then intensified. Then he screamed as he felt the energy drained from his body and felt like he was falling through the bench he was lying on, and right through the floor.

He passed out, and the alien pulled up a chair beside him, and stared at him. It had been sheer serendipity that had brought this one to them, and the alien was contented with his lot as jailer to the powerful man. As a food source, he was unsurpassed. When they had discovered only one being alive on the great ship as it groaned and slowed near their base, the Greys had been disappointed. But when they discovered the identity of that one being, disappointment had turned to delight. The psychic energy that this one held could feed them all telepathically for months on end.

Chapter Five

Laura awoke late at night, around one a.m. She wondered what had awoken her, and then drifted back to sleep. Then in her dream she felt it again; the feeling that had woken her up, the feeling of having every ounce of energy dragged out of her, so that it felt like she was going to drop down through the floor and be swallowed up by the ground beneath the palace. She screamed, and objects flew about the room. The huge black cat, Gan, sat up and looked around, then ducked under the bed as a heavy ornament flew past just by his head and thudded into the far wall, leaving a dent.

Shiva and Zokar came skidding into the room, sideways in the doorway, disruptors raised, then hesitated, looking confused because there was no enemy. Ghrian was hot on their heels, and the huge golden cat crouched behind Zokar and scanned the room with his deep blue eyes, ready to pounce. Zokar stared at Laura, whose eyes were open but blank and terrified, then took ten quick strides across the room and slapped her soundly on the face. She woke up. Ghrian trotted up behind Zokar.

All the objects flying around the room fell to the floor.

"Galaxies, Zokar, take it easy!" growled Shiva, but watched in amazement as the redness faded almost immediately from Laura's face. Zokar knew there would be no bruise.

"She could destroy this palace if we left her asleep and dreaming," pointed out Zokar, "And all of us with it."

Shiva sighed and looked down. Zokar reached over

to Laura. Gently he touched her face, checking that she was really awake, "Are you alright?" he asked her. Ghrian sat at the bedside, looking puzzled, then licked his paws and looked at Zokar thoughtfully. Then he spotted Gan under the bed and crawled under there with him. He turned around awkwardly in the restricted space until both cats were peering out from the blankets overhanging the bed.

She gazed up at Zokar foggily, and asked, "Did you slap me?" her voice was incredulous.

"Yes." The elf did not apologise. He never did. He sighed and realised that his adrenalin-charged body was probably not going to settle down for some time now, and asked, "Coffee, anyone?"

"Yeah," said Shiva sleepily.

There was a long pause, then Zokar pointed out, "I don't make coffee."

"I'm the Captain."

Laura shrugged and grinned, "Not my department."

Zokar rolled his eyes and said loudly, "Computer, get a bot in here with coffees for us all."

"Wow, Zokar made coffee!" exclaimed Shiva.

"The things I do for you," grumbled Zokar.

Ten minutes later the three of them were sitting on the bed, drinking coffee and listening to Laura try to explain the inexplicable.

"It feels like all my energy is being sucked right out of me," she explained, "Like something's just pulling and pulling, like a vacuum cleaner has been put to my head and," she stopped, looking up at Zokar with a confused expression, "I bet you think this just sounds irrational."

"Not at all," answered Zokar, "I have never observed you to be anything but rational. But it is very difficult to describe something which you do not understand yourself, to someone else who has not experienced it."

"Yes," sighed Laura.

Shiva shivered in the low temperature of the room. Zokar and Laura with their elvish blood did not feel the cold so much as the human did. Laura noticed his shivering and dragged an extra blanket from the end of her bed and pulled it around him.

Zokar said to her, "Especially as we don't know why this is happening in your dreams. There is so much we do not understand about you."

"I know," she murmured, as Shiva unselfconsciously wriggled into the slightly warmer space between Zokar's body and her own, bumping against Zokar in a manner for which the elf would have immediately killed anyone else. The elf's eyes flicked to Shiva and back, but otherwise he did not react. Laura handed Shiva another blanket, and then said, "The strange thing is, there is a direction."

"What?" asked Zokar and Shiva in unison, both surprised. "Where?" added Shiva.

She raised her hand and pointed out the window to the night sky, "There."

Zokar summarized thoughtfully, "So you are having irregular dreams, about losing all your energy, and these dreams are coming from a specific direction in space?" He pondered this for a while, staring out into space past the stars of Eridani, a pattern he now recognised easily from Earth. From here in the Solar system, beyond Eridani, lay the distant galaxy of Andromeda.

"Could it be someone else?" asked Shiva, and they both looked at him. He explained further, "Could this energy loss, be happening to someone else, and you're getting, like, sort of their distress calls? You are very sensitive in that area."

Laura nodded slowly, and said to Zokar, "I think that may be it. So, what do we do about it?"

"Do?" asked Zokar, feeling puzzled.

"Your utter and complete lack of a social conscience never ceases to amaze me," grinned Shiva to Zokar.

"My lack of a what?" asked Zokar.

Laura smiled, "I think that a social conscience is as alien a concept to Zokar, as personal space is to you, Shiva."

Shiva moved away from her sulkily, bumping into Zokar again and gaining him an arch look from the elf. Shiva looked at up at Zokar and explained, "It's freezing in here."

"Not many seek me out for my warmth," teased Zokar. Shiva shrugged.

Laura shook her head at them, and asked Shiva, "Well, our dear 'joint conscience,' what do we do about this?"

Shiva looked thoughtful, "Well, I guess we don't have to do anything, but I am curious. So, hell, why don't we just jump in the Reingold and follow your little directional beacon and see where it takes us?"

Laura looked at Zokar for guidance. Zokar pondered for a few moments. The Empress Arlene was expecting the Reingold to set sail for the Core in the next week. She had demanded a conference with Laura to try to start an alliance between the Terrans and the Galactic Union. However, Zokar considered, they couldn't take Laura to the Core in this condition. This needed to be resolved first. Hopefully, it would only add a couple of days to their trip.

Zokar decided to keep his own council about the Empress's parley demand for now. He spoke up. "It would make more sense than waiting here until these nightmares become serious enough that you injure someone. It should only take a day or so of travel to find anyone who is the source of these distress calls, as we are only a short distance from the edge of the galaxy. There is not much of the galaxy left between us and the intergalactic void, in the direction in which you pointed earlier."

"Good point," murmured Shiva, and leaned down to nibble on Laura's shoulder through her nightshirt. She slapped him away, "Shiva!"

"Ow! What was that for?"

"You might have a conscience, but as for decency-"

"What?" he demanded, irritably.

"Zokar is *right there*!" she growled at him.

"So?" grinned Shiva.

"I shall take my leave," smiled Zokar, amused at them both, then stopped at the door. "You cannot prevent her from dreaming forever, Shiva."

"I can try," said Shiva, and as the tall elf turned away laughing, there were shrieks and giggles from behind him in the room. Ghrian realised that Zokar was leaving and bolted out from under the bed, catching him up in the doorway and falling into place behind him.

The two men did not need to talk to each other to convey their thoughts; that Shiva's behaviour was intended to distract Laura from the worrying telepathic impressions.

Zokar arrived back at his cabin, then walked over to the bed and dropped his robe and climbed in under the covers. Over beside the door on a thick mattress, Ghrian curled up and went back to sleep.

The next day, the three of them and Trudi were standing in a shuttle, being ferried up to the waiting Reingold. The massive black and red vessel loomed ever larger in the view screen as they approached it.

"We really should get a smaller ship," suggested Trudi, and both Shiva and Zokar turned to stare at her, looking utterly scandalised.

"What?" she asked.

"I think, Trudi, the Reingold is home to them, just as Earth is to us," suggested Laura.

"Oh," said Trudi.

"Rubbish," snapped Zokar, irritably. He felt even more irritable when no-one took any notice of his tone of voice.

Shiva turned his attention back to the hulking black cylinder of the Reingold, "The new nose-cone looks good. You wouldn't know it wasn't the original."

He and Zokar exchanged a look, then looked at the women. Shiva smiled but said nothing, and Zokar shook his head at the human.

"Actually," said Zokar, "Given Trudi's invention of

the new fighting tactic of ramming the opposition en masse, I have had an additional exterior nose-cone mounted on springs, at either end of the ship."

Shiva chuckled, and Trudi looked embarrassed.

"Knock it off, you two," muttered Laura.

"It worked, didn't it? Saved the planet, I did," said Trudi defiantly, doing a wonderful Yoda-like voice which was lost on the men but made Laura chortle.

Zokar smiled and hugged her, "And with style, from what I heard."

"Is it true you were laughing, when you rammed them?" asked Shiva.

"I was laughing because I was alive, silly. I thought the Reingold would blow up when it hit the other ships, and when it didn't, well... I was *alive*," said Trudi.

"Always a bonus," agreed Zokar, exchanging a look with Shiva.

"I'm glad you didn't blow up my ship," muttered Shiva, earning him a long appraising look from Laura.

The shuttle entered the enormous bay of the Reingold, which could easily have accommodated a Galactic Union battle cruiser, and dwarfed their tiny shuttle. It flew into one of the shuttle docking airlocks, which were designed to accommodate smaller vessels.

"I never noticed that before," commented Trudi, "They don't always pressurize the whole hangar deck?"

"To evacuate and then re-pressurise the entire hangar deck would take an enormous amount of power. These smaller docking bays are designed to use a lot less energy pumping gas around, to allow smaller ships to dock more quickly and efficiently," explained Shiva.

"What happens when you take in a large vessel like a Galactic Union battle cruiser? Do you pressurise the whole deck then?" asked Trudi, ever curious.

Shiva was always happy to talk about his ship. "Not necessarily, although it can be done very quickly if required in a rescue situation. In that case, the larger the ship being taken on board, the less air needed to pressurise around it, because there is simply less volume of free space around the vessel in the hangar. Provided of course, that the ship being rescued still has its own oxygen. Obviously if it does not, then we sometimes pressurise within the salvaged ship too. Sometimes not, if there are no survivors."

"So have you ever pressurised the whole deck?" asked Laura.

Zokar snarled visibly, "Shiva filled the whole hangar deck up with war refugees, once. The noise and stench were unbearable."

Shiva stared at Zokar, "One hundred and sixty three thousand souls, Zokar, and you would have just left them there."

"It did not occur to me to take them with us. They brought nothing of value and consumed three years' worth of supplies in the three days it took to ferry them to safety."

"You see? You see what I have to deal with, every day?" grumbled Shiva to the others. "Zokar, listen to me carefully; letting innocent people die is wrong. It is morally reprehensible, and we don't do that."

"Yes, Captain," Zokar shrugged.

"Unbelievable," murmured Laura.

Trudi was looking very thoughtful, and asked, "So, you could fit a whole Union Battle Cruiser in this hold?"

"Yes," said Shiva, proudly.

Zokar looked curiously at Trudi, who was looking very thoughtful indeed.

When they left the shuttle, Shiva walked slowly to allow the two women and spoke quietly to Zokar, "You were one of those war refugees."

"That's beside the point. You should not have rescued us."

"I should have let you and all your people die?"

"It would have been the rational choice," said Zokar indifferently, with a shrug.

Chapter Six

The Empress Arlene's voice was a snarl as she stared at the screen, "You are going where?"

Zokar's demeanour was indifferent, glacial almost, "To the outer rim. We will be a few days, perhaps a week at most, Your Eminence."

Arlene suggested, "Do not play games with me, Zokar. You have a hostage to fortune, well within my grasp."

"Your Eminence, any move on your part to take action in that direction would result in a permanently unsettled galactic situation."

Shiva overrode Zokar smoothly, "Shiva Kiran, here, Your Eminence."

"Ah, yes. My erstwhile daughter's lapdog," said the Empress sweetly.

Shiva stiffened up and Zokar stepped forward angrily. The Empress smiled even more sweetly. The human and the elf glared at her and Shiva whispered savagely, "What do you want?"

"If she is not here in five days I send the fleet looking for her," snapped the Empress imperiously, and cut the transmission.

Zokar looked at Shiva, and Shiva snapped, "Elesk, you have the con. I'm going to discuss strategies with Zokar and Laura."

He made it into the thankfully soundproof lift before snapping.

"Arrogant cow! What did she mean, you have a hostage to fortune, Zokar? What was that about?"

"It is nothing, it was an empty threat. It appears that we will be risking another attack by the Galactic Union if we take Laura to find the source of these nightmares. How is she faring?"

"Not well. The nightmares are getting worse, Zokar. Last night I barely dodged a computer terminal flying past my head."

"Her state of mind is becoming a grave risk to you, Shiva," observed Zokar.

"So what, we have a choice between risking a Galactic Union invasion, and me putting up with a few of her nightmares? I think it's a no-brainer, Zokar."

"No, you need to take these nightmares of hers very seriously. She could kill you. She could explode this ship in her sleep and kill us all. We must find and eliminate the source of her nightmares, and quickly. I would rather take my chances with the Galactic Union fleet than face her in a week's time if we do nothing."

Shiva pursed his lips, "I guess…"

"Also, if we do not have Laura in a fit mental state, we cannot repel the Galactic Union fleet," added Zokar.

"You're right, old friend. I'm sorry. Arlene's attitude threw me."

"She is used to unquestioning obedience. Your refusal to cooperate upset her."

"I can't believe she's Laura's mother. What a nasty piece of work!"

"You may be looking into a crystal ball, Shiva. In a hundred years, Laura may be exactly like that."

"No chance!" retorted Shiva.

"You do not know the pressures of ruling, or what they might do to her mind."

"I can't believe that. I could never think that of her. I'd leave her if I thought that she was that kind of person."

Zokar chuckled, "You don't seriously think that you have a choice of backing out of this relationship if it does not suit you, Shiva? Please tell me, you are not so deluded as all

37

that?"

"Why? What's she gonna do, melt my brain?"

Zokar raised his eyebrows, "That is one of many options, I suppose."

"No, come on Zokar, you don't-" but the human's blue eyes looked up into Zokar's and something in them obviously gave him pause.

The elf said angrily, "I have warned you again and again that she is dangerous. You will not listen."

"I'm not planning on leaving her, Zokar."

"Do not. You are, as I believe her mother put it, 'her lapdog'."

Zokar felt a sudden impact on his ear and realised that Shiva had reached up and swatted him, which was no mean feat considering the elf had a good ten centimetres on him in height. "Don't kid yourself," said Shiva.

"And you are also my lapdog," grinned Zokar, feeling mischievous. Another blow, much harder, struck his other ear, and Zokar protested mildly, with a slight warning tone, "Ow."

"Not at all, quite the opposite," grinned Shiva, "Anyone else hit you like that, you'd have knocked them down."

Zokar shrugged and smiled as they arrived in Shiva's quarters and corrected his captain, "No, I would have vapourised them."

They opened the door and a chair flew out and smashed against the far wall of the corridor.

Another chair followed it, heading straight for Shiva's head, but Zokar reached over and snatched it out of the air in front of Shiva's nose.

Shiva darted in ahead of Zokar, and grabbed Laura by both wrists, "Wake up!" he cried, shaking her, and her eyes flew open. Around the room, about fifty objects dropped abruptly to the floor. Zokar had walked around behind her and supported her as she rose from the bed. Gan crawled sheepishly out from under the bed where he had been hiding from the disturbance.

"Damn," she whispered, looking around the room at the mess.

Zokar stepped over to the communications unit, "Elesk," he called and waited for her efficient acknowledgment moments later, "Set course for the Outer Rim, and give us maximum speed, please."

"Aye sir. Do we follow the heading you and Laura gave us earlier?"

Zokar said, "Yes." He snapped off the communications link and looked at Laura and Shiva, nibbling anxiously at his lower lip.

"That's going to upset Mommy Dearest," observed Shiva dryly.

"Oh, so you met my new mother?"

Shiva lowered big eyes onto her.

"Sweet, isn't she?" asked Laura, so that Shiva chuckled and then Zokar surprised them both by giving one of his rare, deep chuckles.

Shiva stared at Zokar, and asked, "Is there something you're not telling us?"

But then his attention was caught by the odd expression on Laura's face. She was staring transfixed at the wall of the cabin, back in the direction of Earth. Shiva asked, "Laura?"

She did not answer at first, then whispered, "Help me," very softly.

"What?" asked Zokar, looking at Laura.

She turned to him, then turned back to the wall and whispered, "Don't leave me here." Her eyes were wide and unblinking.

Shiva grabbed her arms, "Laura!"

She snapped out of it suddenly, and shook her head, "We shouldn't leave Earth."

Zokar threw his eyes up to the ceiling then looked to Shiva.

Shiva looked worried, but concealed it quickly,

"Here's what we're going to do, Lor. We'll go sort out this beacon of yours and find out who's behind it, then we'll head straight for the Core and sort out that witch of a mother of yours, okay? Earth will be fine."

"How do you know that?" she asked him, not defiantly but curiously.

"I feel it in my bones. Call it a hunch," shrugged Shiva.

Zokar stared at him, then said to Laura, who was looking extremely reluctant, "You should go with his plan. Shiva does not have hunches often, but when he does they're *always* right."

"I thought he was the non-psychic one amongst us," protested Laura.

"Totally. He is an anomaly," agreed Zokar. "But he is an anomaly whose hunches are always right."

"When did you notice that?" asked Shiva. "I only just noticed it myself recently."

Zokar shrugged and said, "The last time you saved my life, it was because you followed a hunch. It brought to mind your previous hunches and I noticed a consistent pattern."

"Oh."

Laura blinked at them both, "'The last time' you saved his life? What, it happens every day?"

"Sometimes," agreed Shiva, but even he looked a little disturbed by the conversation. He disliked any mention of his deficiencies in the psychic field, because it pointed to a weakness, which was not a good thing in Shiva's mind. Why should he, the most human of them all, be so completely lacking in this one important talent?

Up on the bridge, Trudi watched entranced at the amazing sight of Saturn, its dusky rings bright and shining in the now-distant light of Sol, swinging majestically past on the view screens as they headed out of the Solar system. The golden light of the giant planet lit her face and reflected off her dark, glossy hair.

Back at the Core, Arlene stared coldly at the messenger before her, "They're what?"

"They are heading for the Rim, Your Eminence, at maximum hyperdrive."

She shook her head with disbelief, "They're running away?"

"It would appear so, Your Eminence."

She was still shaking her head, "I can't believe that; not of Zokar."

"Perhaps you frightened Laura, my Lady?" asked a deep voice behind her.

Arlene turned to look at the tall, silver haired elf behind her. "Ataar. What are you doing out here?"

"I came to see what was happening."

She pursed her lips, and said thoughtfully, "I am afraid our friends are trying a little subterfuge. I do not believe any of this. I do not believe that the Reingold, nor its captain, nor its first officer, nor my daughter would flee. This is a trick."

She steepled her fingers, and decided, "They are playing for time… a diversion. They must be manufacturing more ships or weapons. Deploy the fleet."

"No," whispered Ataar, closing his eyes briefly. Ataar, a child of war, was sucked suddenly back into memories of the desolation and violence which had surrounded him and robbed him of his childhood. Of pain, constant gnawing hunger, rolling grief as friend after friend after brother after sister perished around him, and then as planet after planet was destroyed. He shuddered and stared miserably at Arlene.

She ignored him.

"Send five thousand ships to Earth, and ready my ship. I will lead the remainder to follow the Reingold and bring her back. If I have to clap her in irons and use her psychic abilities to help me defend the Core, I will," said Arlene, cold and efficient now that war was upon her.

41

Ataar remained silent and dejected as they headed back to their chambers. His wife was, above all, a warrior queen, but he suspected that her daughter was the one being who had the will to oppose Arlene and make all their lives a living hell for many decades to come.

Chapter Seven

On the Reingold's bridge, Gan snarled suddenly from near the captain's chair, and Ghrian sat up from his normal sleeping place next to Zokar. Shiva stared at Gan, then glanced back at Ghrian.

"Captain," the helmsman's voice had a note in it. Instantly Shiva and Zokar were sitting up, alert and edgy.

"Report."

"Sir, ten... seventeen.... no... thirty-four Galactic Union patrol vessels just left their assigned patrol areas and are now apparently pursuing the Reingold. The closest is five light years behind us, and the body of the group is ten light years behind that."

"Evasive action! Red alert, all systems to maximum, charge all weapons, standby crews to shuttles. Power up main shields, shut down recreational systems and divert power to sensors," rattled off Shiva, and glanced up at Zokar, a nod all the response he needed to know that Zokar's people were ready.

A howling alarm sounded throughout the ship and all hands darted about to their stations. Down in her bunk, Laura sat bolt upright at the sound of the alarm, then grabbed her clothes and began getting dressed.

"Closing, three light years now," the helmsman was getting nervous. The Reingold was a big ship, and that meant that it took a while to power her up to achieve full hyperdrive. The patrol ships were small scouts, fast, well-armed, high powered and dangerous if too many of them got too close.

"Steady," murmured Zokar, so that the younger

crewmembers heard his deep voice and focused on their readouts. Shiva heard too, and shot the elf a quick grateful look. Zokar was holding his hand up and then dropped it, and said, "Hyperdrive at full power.... *now*."

Shiva was talking over him as soon as Zokar's hand started moving, "Go! Full hyperdrive. Get us out of here, mister!" The captain stood and slammed his fist onto the helm console just as laser fire from the Galactic Union battleships started erupting about the ship.

The Reingold went into hyperdrive, obliterating two of the smaller vessels which had ventured too close to survive the temporo-spatial disruption of the huge vessel suddenly slamming at full power along the wormhole.

Shiva sat back in his chair, then swung around to face Zokar, "Good work."

Zokar nodded, but waited for more, and was not surprised when Shiva came out with another barrage of commands that took some of the younger crew by surprise. They ran around, following his orders, continuing to set the Reingold up for transiting hostile space.

Laura arrived on the bridge quietly, and walked up behind Shiva's chair, putting a hand on his shoulder, "Do you need me?" she asked quietly, in response to which Shiva put a hand up on hers gratefully but shook his head, "Nothing we can't handle conventionally, Lor, but you could grab a chair up there by Zokar if you want. You never know."

"What happened?" she asked.

Shiva turned to her and said quietly, "The Galactic Union appears to have mobilised against us."

She had sat down in the chair that Zokar swung around for her, but she said, "Oh no.... Earth."

"One would presume that Earth has also been targeted," said Zokar solemnly. He continued to work on his console, but his ears flattened to listen to Shiva and Laura talking behind him.

"And I'm not there," sighed Laura.

Zokar shot her a look which clearly said, *pull yourself*

together, but Shiva spoke more clearly, mostly for the benefit of the new Terran members of his crew, "Earth is well defended, Laura. They'll stand. Don't forget the Union ships have to get past the fleet and the system defences before they get anywhere near Earth, then there's the Peregrine device and the group mentality. Earth will be fine."

Laura didn't look convinced, and asked, "How much speed can we get out of this rig, Shiva? And why weren't we cloaked?"

"This much speed. And cloaking uses up a lot of energy, which would be wasted. The new Galactic Union battle cruiser sensors can detect us anyway."

She said, "We're still heading for the Rim?"

Shiva nodded, then asked her, "Is our heading still accurate? We haven't overshot the mark yet?"

There was silence for a few seconds, and Zokar glanced over at her. She looked as though she were focusing inwards, then stared out the front of the vessel, directly in line with their course, "We are still on course, but-"

"What?" asked Zokar.

"Even at maximum speed, it's still a good five days travel out that way."

"My Lady," the helmsman looked dubious, "That puts us well beyond the Rim and into the intergalactic void. Are you sure there's something out there?"

"Oh, yes," she said, clearly, "It's there all right."

"What is?" asked Shiva, "Can you tell us yet?"

"No, but I'm starting to wonder if the Reingold is going to have the range to get us there," she said, and Zokar saw a worried frown crease Shiva's forehead. Even Zokar felt a qualm at the thought of running out of fuel in the Void. It was a death that even the seasoned warrior elf found a daunting prospect. A quick death in battle was one thing, but starving, freezing or running out of oxygen did not appeal to Zokar at all. He met Shiva's eyes briefly and saw the same expression there that he knew must be in his own eyes.

45

Far behind the Reingold, the small Galactic Union patrol ships were quickly overtaken by huge, sleek vessels. The new Galactic Union battle cruisers were still forbidding, grey hulks, but unlike the old Union cruisers, were sleek and streamlined, like giant sharks. The ships headed out along the last known course of the Reingold.

"Where are they going?" asked the captain of one of the leading vessels, studying the scanner readings of the Reingold's path, "They're just heading out into the Void."

"It would appear so, sir," said his first officer.

"Call for twenty tankers. That damned vessel has got three weeks' fuel supply on us. They could get far enough out to run us out of fuel then just sail back past us and we'd be drifting dead in space. Get the tankers and set up a supply line using those older patrol ships as tugs for the fuel holds. They're not quick enough to fight the Reingold, we might as well use them for something."

"Aye sir," said the first officer and went back to her station to begin organising the supply chain.

"Sir," said the helmsman to the captain dubiously, "What if they're making a run for Andromeda? They're heading that way."

The captain stared at him, "There's no way. They wouldn't have the fuel."

"Not with Union technology, sir, but during the last war, we've seen what the Terrans have done. Is it possible they could have developed more efficient systems and be heading for Andromeda?"

The captain looked thoughtfully at the young helmsman, "In that old hulk? It's possible, lieutenant. But it's not likely."

"What do we do then, sir?"

"Why, let them go, son. We can't chase them off the edge of the world, now, can we?"

"Sir?"

"Joke, son."

"Oh. But you are serious about letting them go."

The first officer spoke up, "Even with ten thousand fuel tankers we couldn't make the crossing to Andromeda, helmsman. We would have no choice. If their technology's that good, we'll just have to let them go and thank our lucky stars they haven't put their expertise into long range weaponry instead, and haven't blown us out of space by now instead of just running away."

"We hope," muttered the captain in response, giving his first officer a meaningful glance. He knew the Reingold may have simply chosen to wait until they were hopelessly far out in the Void before disabling them with some new form of weaponry and leaving them to die. But he didn't see any reason to point that out to the junior crew members, and the senior ones would have figured it out for themselves by now, so he merely said, "Meanwhile, our orders are to pursue and destroy the Reingold if possible, and that is what we will do."

"Aye, Sir."

Back on the Reingold, Zokar caught a slight movement in the chair next to him, and with elvish speed caught Laura as she fainted. Shiva was up to the chair in a heartbeat, but said "We can't give over the bridge, Zokar. Call Trudi and the medics for her."

"Shiva, it might be wise to sedate her. She cannot direct us in this state, and she may start having those violent dreams again."

Shiva looked worried, but agreed, "Alright."

Trudi arrived in minutes, looking grim and a little frightened, two hefty nurses at her side, and Zokar handed Laura over to the bigger of the two nurses, gave Trudi a reassuring smile, and said, "Look after her. Sedate her to stop her from dreaming. The ship is in no immediate danger."

Zokar knew that Trudi was not a seasoned crewmember and that the alarms and sudden flurry of ship-wide activity would probably have frightened her. He remembered the first few skirmishes when he had first come aboard the Reingold. He had been deep in the bowels of the ship, knowing nothing about the decisions being made or the success or failure of the battle, until the sirens ceased and he assumed they were going to survive. That was provided of course, there was neither a slow leak in the hull nor a fatal structural flaw in the ship's skeleton from the battle. It had not been a nice feeling, and he remembered the relief that he had felt when he was finally allowed to accompany the captain to the bridge, where he could see what was going on and where he knew, to some extent, whether the next second was going to be his last or whether he was going to live to fight another artificial ship's day. Zokar, cool and calculated as he was in most matters, could not stand the feeling of not knowing what was going on around him. He would rather be in the thick of battle relying on his own wits and strength, than trust anyone else's.

The Reingold howled on through the void, howling because inside a ship there is atmosphere and the ear can detect the strange vibrations of the hull being buffeted and flung through the wormhole that is hyperdrive. Those vibrations come straight from the groaning hull, through the ship's interior atmosphere, to the ear, and are especially noticeable when the captain knows the Galactic Union is on his tail, so is pushing the ship to give everything she has and more.

Zokar watched Shiva sit back in his command chair. The elf knew that his captain's mind would be racing faster than the ship, and that Shiva was sitting back so that his peripheral vision would encompass every possible light and panel visible from his chair. Zokar also knew from long experience that Shiva would be relying on the elf to regularly scan the ones that he knew his captain could not see, in case the junior crew members missed a light or a tell-tale at a vital moment. So Zokar performed his allotted tasks patiently, scanning the lights and tell-tales within his purview.

The younger crew members on the bridge glanced occasionally at the senior members of the command crew, taking heart from their calmness.

Four hours later, Zokar stepped down to the central console, "We have put sufficient distance between us. I would suggest rest for both of us. Tomorrow may be a long day, captain."

Shiva nodded, and said, "I'm going to check on Laura and get some sleep."

Chapter Eight

Something had changed in the dark-haired man's limited world. There was a commotion, and then a sudden absence of supervision. The machines that held him also drained his energy, constantly. But now, his jailers were distracted. They left the machines running, but all went off to investigate something else. It must have been something very distracting, because they did not leave the machines on full power. That was a dangerous thing to do, for they were calibrated so that full power matched the normal maximum output of energy from his mind. When they were left on less than full power, his energy was not drained quickly enough, and soon started to build back up towards functional levels.

He regained consciousness, and slowly sat up. He focused on the restraints, and gradually they glowed blue, then the glow diminished and eventually they dissolved into thin air. He lifted his legs over the side of the slab that he was lying on, and felt the stiffness in his limbs, the soreness of horrendous bed sores. He focused for a few minutes on reducing them. The stiffness and soreness abated, his injuries healed within a few seconds and his body was quickly restored to its normal functioning state. He destroyed the internal workings of the machines so they could no longer draw his power. Then his mind reached out....

On the Reingold, Laura St James' mind tore itself loose from the moorings of the heavy sedatives and she sat bolt upright in her bunk and whispered, "My God!"

Shiva, sitting in the chair next to the bunk, sat up too, and asked, "Wha-" foggily.

"Shiva! I'm getting something really clear now. The presence we are looking for is that way!" she said, pointing and then hesitated, "And I think they're being held prisoner."

She stared at Shiva, who had finally woken up fully, as had Gan.

"Do you have any idea who or what they are?" asked Shiva sleepily.

She hesitated, her eyes taking on an intense concentration, then shook her head, frustrated, "I can't tell. It's a powerful pull, though, now."

Shiva sighed. First they were off on some wild goose chase after Laura's phantoms, out in the Void, then the Galactic Union had taken offence at their actions and was pursuing them, then Laura had second thoughts about leaving Earth, now she wanted to chase the phantoms again. Shiva did not doubt for a moment that she was right though: that there was a strongly telepathic presence out there, calling to her.

Back on the space station, the man collapsed to the floor in the doorway of his cell as a large group of Greys ran up the corridor towards him and their big, black, liquid eyes all fastened on to his as their minds began to draw his power from him. They carried him back to his slab and found more restraints, locking him back into place. They ramped the machines back up to full power. A group of Greys stayed in the next room as a backup draw on his power.

Back on the Reingold, Laura sighed and said to Shiva, "It's gone. I've lost him again."

"Him? You mean one man has been the source of all these nightmares?" asked Shiva.

"I think so. But Shiva, these are *Greys*."

Shiva was wide awake now, "What?"

"What I saw, in the contact; I think he's being held by *Greys*. I think they've kidnapped him. Shiva, they're supposed to be our allies, but this person doesn't seem to think they are."

"If he knows of the Greys, does he also know of Earth? Maybe he's being held by a renegade group of Greys?"

"Maybe." But she didn't look utterly convinced, Shiva noticed.

"Who is he, Laura?" Shiva asked, but only got a confused shake of her head in response.

Chapter Nine

The Reingold continued to flee the Galactic Union fleet, and soon passed outside the galaxy.

The supertankers that the Galactic Union had requested soon arrived. They were towed out in a thin line from the rim, the first few strung like sparkling beads along the line of pursuit in the starlight, but the rest lost in the deep darkness of the Void.

Trudi arrived on the Reingold bridge, holding a fist full of mind-shields, and walked up to Laura, "I have an idea, Lor. Try one of these."

"Why? I won't be able to do anything with that on," said Laura.

"Yes, but maybe whatever's bugging you won't be able to get through either?"

Laura shrugged and slipped one of the mind-shields on over her blonde hair. She frowned, "It feels weird. I can't...." but then she stilled and said, "That does feel better, thanks, Tru."

Trudi was already wearing one of the devices, and took one over to Shiva, "Try this," she suggested. Shiva frowned, but took one of the headpieces and slipped it onto his head. He looked thoughtful, then shook his head and pulled it off, "It doesn't seem to make any difference to me, Trudi."

Trudi nodded, took the device back and offered it to Zokar, who shook his head and said, "No need, Trudi. Elves are practically psi-null."

She nodded and took the device back from Zokar,

saying quietly, "I don't understand why it doesn't affect Shiva, though. He's human."

"Yes, it is odd, but from everything I have seen, he is psi-null too. A rarity, in a human," replied Zokar quietly, trying not to let Shiva hear.

"This is helping, Trudi," said Laura, "Perhaps you should offer them to all the humans on board?"

"Okay, I'll get right onto it," smiled Trudi and left the bridge.

Zokar wandered down to the captain's chair, and Shiva said quietly, "I heard what you said. It seems we have something in common."

"There is no shame in being psi-null, Shiva. My whole species is practically psi-null," Zokar's voice was low.

"Yes, but I pride myself in being human. It makes me feel not so human, for the first time in my life."

Zokar sighed, searching for something to say, but could think of nothing. Instead he just stood quietly beside his captain, gazing into the disconcerting blackness of the void. It was disorientating, to have no frame of reference such as passing stars or asteroids. It felt like they were floating dead still in space, but this impression was belied by the readouts which showed that the Reingold's engines were moving her along at maximum hyperdrive.

Shiva flicked the view screen to a reverse view, and they watched silently as the edges of their own galaxy gradually contracted in from the sides of the view screen. Shiva watched the shrinking galaxy for a few moments longer, then Zokar was glad when he toggled the view back to the Void before them; somehow the elf found even the deep blackness less disconcerting.

Shiva said, "You could fly like this for a thousand years and never know you were moving."

"Hmm," said Zokar, "When will we know when we have arrived at our destination, if Laura's mind is shielded?"

"There will be something there, Zokar. We've been following the same straight vector since we left the Solar system. If we just keep following this heading, we'll come to whatever it is she sensed."

The elf nodded, but did not look that certain. Then he jumped as Trudi touched his arm, "What?"

"I have an idea for upgrading our cloaking systems," said Trudi.

Shiva nodded at them both, "Engineering. Go. Keep me informed."

Chapter Ten

On the third day, the almost-forgotten towering polarizer on the engineering deck of the Reingold, not far from the bridge, hummed into life automatically, protecting the engines from some power drain that the automatic sensors had detected in the space around the great vessel.

On the bridge, Gan and Ghrian both sat up and growled.

Zokar reported to his Captain, "The protective polarizer on the engineering deck has just activated, sir." He continued, "Coming up on something. Long range scanners are picking up a space station. Large, with seventy three vessels around it. It appears to be what set off the protective polariser."

"That's odd. Go to silent running. Cloak us. What are the dimensions of the station? What's its firepower?" asked Shiva.

Zokar replied, "Cloaking now, sir. The space station is six thousand metres in diameter, and appears to have minimal defensive weaponry. The vessels are long range scout models, each equipped with the equivalent of our scout class defensive guns."

Shiva turned to Laura, who was sitting up near Zokar. "Laura, are you getting anything? Is this it?"

She had taken off the slim headband, and her face was a study in concentration, then she sagged in her chair. Trudi ran over and quickly replaced the mind shield, and said, "Something around here is acting exactly like that suppression generator Laura blew up when we first left Earth. It's draining her."

"Good thing we've got these," said the helmsman, tapping his headband.

"Hmm," said Shiva, "Good thing indeed, but it means Laura and the other Terrans can't help us if anything goes wrong."

Elesk looked up from her position next to Zokar at the science station, "Sir, those life form readings, the ship configurations.... these are Greys, sir."

Shiva looked at Laura, "So, you were right: they *are* Greys."

Laura nodded anxiously, "And I don't think they're friendlies, Shiva."

He nodded, then turned to his crew, "These are Greys, but they may not be friendlies. We'll stay cloaked, but try hailing that base before the Union fleet catches up with us. We'll see what response we get. Keep it on a tight beam though, directional to the Grey base. We don't want those Union ships behind us picking up our signals."

"Aye, sir," replied the round-faced communications officer. His voice became part of the background noise, "Galactic Trade Alliance ship Reingold to Grey base, do you read me?" He repeated the message over and over, and several variations of it, but to no avail. Eventually he shrugged at Shiva and said sadly, "Sorry, sir, they're not responding."

"Are they getting our signal?" asked Shiva.

"Sensors say yes they are, sir."

"Why aren't they answering?" pondered Shiva.

A thousand possibilities rushed through Zokar's mind: was the station even manned? Were they hostiles? Had there been a plague? Had the Union already been out here and attacked them? Was that why the Union had hunted after them so furiously so far? Perhaps they didn't want the Reingold having a look at the Grey base? He shook his head at his captain, "Too many possibilities to say at this stage, sir."

Shiva turned to Zokar, "Come on, let's shuttle over

there. We'll go in ready for hostilities, just in case. The humans can't help us on this one, so it looks like we're going to have to do it the old-fashioned way. Zokar, I want an assault team of thirty to shuttle bay one." He reached under his command chair for his utility belt, swords and disruptor.

Zokar grinned and followed suit, grabbing a powerful bow, two long swords, and a few other odds and ends from under his console. He leaned over his console, hit a button and said, "Assault team, crew members eleven through forty, to shuttle bay one. Shuttle pilots fifty-five and sixty-one. "

Laura and Trudi stood up to go with them, and Zokar nodded at Elesk, who stepped across into the central chair smoothly as they all left for the shuttle hangar. Gan and Ghrian trotted at their masters' heels.

As they walked through the corridors, Shiva nodded at Laura and Trudi and said to Zokar, "We're going on muscle on this trip, Zokar."

"We have muscle: twenty elves, ten men, and two… cats. The women might slow us down, though."

Laura gave him a dark look and said, "Dad had us taught martial arts. And don't forget Trudi was a police woman. She knows a bit about hand to hand fighting."

The men looked at Trudi, who was rolling up her sleeves and took out a pair of soft leather half gloves and put them on. Then she reached into her jacket pocket, pulled out a pair of nunchucks, flipped them around expertly, and tucked them into her belt. Zokar raised his eyebrows at Shiva with a smug smile.

"Stay out of trouble," Shiva warned Laura.

"How? We're with *you*," she retorted.

Shiva opened his mouth to say something, but obviously thought better of it.

They met with the assault team and filed into the shuttle, which took off immediately. They had no time to waste with the Union fleet approaching rapidly. Trudi handed out mind shields to the three human crewmembers who didn't already have them. Gan and Ghrian presented their heads to her and she looked surprised, but then hooked headbands awkwardly around their ears too.

The Reingold hovered, main guns pointed at the space station, as the shuttle travelled over and docked, without incident.

"I don't like this," muttered Shiva.

They all pinned themselves back against the walls of the shuttle as the doors opened. There was a moment's silence, then disruptor fire erupted about them. The commandos formed a diamond shaped phalanx around Laura, Shiva, Zokar and Trudi.

It was a battle for every inch. At every intersection they had to half-carry Laura for several steps as she whipped off the mind shield for enough seconds to nod in a certain direction, then sagged and needed to be dragged along by Zokar and Shiva for a few seconds until she put the shield back on her head.

Behind them, Trudi walked backwards, using her nunchucks whenever necessary to protect their backs. The big cats walked backwards at her side, dispatching any Greys that came too close.

They came deeper and deeper into the bowels of the station, then klaxons sounded throughout the station and the Greys began to run away from the group, off towards the outer shell of the station.

Shiva pursed his lips and said grimly, "That must be the Union fleet arriving. Dammit! I hoped we'd be gone before they got here!"

With the Grey numbers diminished, their progress was easier. They soon found a large spherical chamber, with a single remaining guard and a single slab. Zokar shot the guard. A prisoner was chained on the slab.

Laura ran over to the slab and stopped, staring open-mouthed at the prisoner there. Shiva walked over quickly then looked puzzled, "Isn't that-?"

Zokar walked over to the slab and looked down at the prisoner, and felt the breath leave his body. "By the Galaxy," he whispered, and quickly undid the restraints on the man's wrists, forehead and ankles, "...Dom!"

It wasn't until Zokar glanced up that he saw the puzzled look that Shiva was giving him, and remembered to wipe the emotions off his elvish face. Shiva raised both eyebrows at Zokar, who ignored him and hefted the unconscious Dom up over his shoulder. Zokar heard a noise outside the room they were in. He spun and dropped to one knee, using his disruptor to fell a group of Greys in the corridor before them. "Let's get out of here."

Zokar noticed that Dom remained unconscious, and Laura seemed dizzy and disorientated, even with the mind shields. He got on the communications link to Elesk as Trudi dizzily pulled a mind shield out of her pocket and put it on Dom's head. He moaned and stirred, but did not awaken.

They left the room, Shiva bringing up the rear. Suddenly a hatch opened behind them and six Greys came pouring out and ran towards Shiva. He turned to face them, and they all pounced on him, grabbing him with their sucker-like arms and smiling evilly at him, their big dark eyes locking onto his. Then they started looking worried, and Shiva laughed and said "Sorry, guys, that doesn't work on me. Nothing to suck on." He pulled out a knife and began slashing his way out of their grip. The Greys gave ear-splitting shrieks as he sliced their arms and legs off. Shiva ran out the door to catch up with the others, who had stopped and were just turning back, prepared to defend Shiva.

"Problem?" asked Zokar.

"Nothing I couldn't handle," grinned Shiva, but then he looked at the swaying bodies of the other humans in the team, and whipped out his communicator, "Elesk, we're losing them: all the humans, and Dom and Laura. Something's wrong; they're not functioning properly."

"Tell me about it!" exclaimed Elesk, who had stepped up to weapons and was frantically helping the gunner to protect the Reingold, "Get back on board quickly, Zokar, I have a feeling that there's something about this enclave that's affecting all the humans among us. And did you just say Dom? Who's Dom?"

"Domhan Keallach," explained Shiva.

The communications unit fell silent.

Shiva went on, "It should take us the same amount of time as it took to get here, to fight our way back, maybe a bit less. Get ready to cover the shuttle as soon as you see it move. What's happening with the Union fleet?"

Elesk's voice sounded shaken, "They're here, but the Grey ships went out and are keeping them back from the station. I think the Union ships are in worse trouble than we are. With any luck, you'll be back on board before the Union ships get past the Greys."

"Good work, Elesk."

They made it, barely. Zokar and Shiva between them had a dozen new wounds that would likely scar, and the team was a mess of broken limbs and injuries.

"Medical bay?" asked Laura, as they exited the shuttle, and Zokar shot her a startled look, "No, back to the bridge. The medics will find us."

They dragged themselves to the bridge, and Zokar put Dom down in a chair near his station, then stood behind the captain's chair, holding his own arm to stem the flow of blood from an injury on his wrist. A medic found him and began fussing over him, and Zokar released his arm and watched the battle between the Union forces and the Greys unfold behind them as they fled.

As the Reingold made its way out from the Grey enclave, Dom regained consciousness and stared fuzzily at Laura, "Laura?"

Then he turned to Zokar and stared at the elf. Zokar shot him the briefest of warning glances, and Dom said nothing, but Zokar saw gratitude flit in the dark eyes of the Empress's son before the look was shuttered over.

"Can you hide us?" suggested Zokar to Laura and Dom.

Dom turned to Laura and said groggily, "Use

61

temporal phasing. It's the only thing that will work."

She shook her head, not understanding, so he reached up, took her hand and said, "Like this."

Laura's face cleared, and nothing happened, but the fire from the Galactic Union and the Greys suddenly seemed to be missing them completely.

"What did you do?" asked Shiva, sounding curious.

"We're two seconds ahead of when we were," explained Dom, sounding distracted.

"Temporal phasing as a cloaking technique. Crude, but effective," said Zokar approvingly.

The temporally shifted Reingold moved along unharmed, and the crew watched as the Grey ships decimated the union fleet. Eventually seven small Union scout ships and fighters managed to escape and flee towards the rim, struggling along far behind the Reingold.

"They'll never make it," said Zokar, then shrugged and turned to the helmsman, "Get us out of here, whatever power you can muster."

"Belay that," came Shiva's quiet voice, "Pick up those Union survivors."

Zokar walked over to Shiva, who had two medics patching him up, and whispered tightly, "You have got to be joking."

"No," murmured Shiva, with a slight lift of his eyebrow at the elf. Zokar pursed his lips, nodded, then moved quickly to comply with his orders.

Laura smiled quietly, and looked at Dom, who was staring at her.

He said, "You came back for me?"

"You did the same for me," she smiled, "And for a helluva lot longer."

Dom looked at each of them in turn, and said to Zokar, "Hey, Zokar."

"Hello," the elf's response was terse.

"He was injured, on the Reingold, remember?" Laura reminded Dom, "You helped him."

"Yes, of course I remember," Dom said, and glanced to Shiva, then back at Zokar. Zokar could practically feel Shiva's eyes burning into the back of his neck.

Laura introduced them, "Dom, I'd like you to meet Captain Shiva Kiran."

"You run this ship?" Dom asked Shiva.

Shiva smiled, "I try to." He winced as the medic poured a silver elvish remedy along the long burn of a disruptor hit on his arm, then stared at his arm as the silver liquid started smoking and his arm started to heal rapidly. The only disadvantage to the quick healing remedies was that they left jagged scars which had to wait for later treatment, which Shiva and Zokar never seemed to have time for. And they hurt like hell.

Dom turned to Zokar, "So this is your captain, the one that was lost on Earth? I am pleased that you found him."

"You knew about me?" asked Shiva curiously. Zokar kept his eyes firmly on his console.

Dom and Laura looked at them both, and both chuckled, because anyone who had known Zokar when he was searching for Shiva, lost on Earth, knew within minutes of meeting Zokar that he had lost his captain and would turn the galaxy upside down in order to find him.

"Yes, and I am pleased to finally meet you all," said Dom quietly, and added, "Thank you for coming to get me. And now, we have a much greater problem than the Galactic Union heading for Earth."

Laura turned to him and asked, "The Greys? But they're our allies."

"No. They are your keepers. You are like prize cattle to them," said Dom, shaking his head, "Come, walk with me, I will explain." He took Laura by the arm and they left the bridge, deep in discussion. Zokar saw Trudi give Shiva a puzzled look, then ducked his head away as she turned to stare at him.

Chapter Eleven

They collected the survivors in the remaining Galactic Union ships, who were all stunned and drained.

Dom explained as Laura led him towards her quarters, "Even at a distance, the Greys draw energy from any human mind. It feels like your legs are suddenly giving out under you. It feels like the floor is sucking you into it, that you are going to sink into the ground and disappear. They are psychic parasites, Laura."

She shuddered, "So that is why they seem peaceful. They would not want to physically harm humans, because they want them kept alive, so they can feed off them?"

"Yes. They have been on your planet for some years, I understand?"

"Since before I arrived there, from what I have gathered, Dom. There was a crash landing in the Nevada desert back in 1947, in a place called Roswell. It's called Area 51. There's some kind of space-time depression or corridor that leads there: my escape pod crashed there too."

"Yes, the rotation of the planet causes... never mind, it's complicated, but you are right, there is a hyperspace contour line leading into that particular site. I noticed it when we were scanning Earth last time I was there."

"When you rescued me."

He grimaced, "I think you had already done a good job of rescuing yourself before I arrived there."

"You did save me from being blown up by that battle cruiser. You saved Zokar, too."

"Yes, of course. I could not leave *him* to die."

She did not notice the strange emphasis he put on that

particular word, because she was absorbed in thought about the Greys.

"So, that explains why humans were so spooked by the Greys, even back in the 1940's and 50's? This telepathic parasitism?" she asked.

"Yes. However, with the suppression generator operating, the Greys could not function sufficiently to draw much energy from their human victims. In addition, back then, their human victims were not functioning fully telepathically anyway, due to the operation of the suppression generator."

"Why do they like Earth people so much?" asked Trudi.

"It is because Terrans have much more powerful minds than humans from the rest of the galaxy, on the whole," explained Dom. He stopped outside her cabin, then asked suddenly, "Can we eat? I'm famished."

"Oh, of course, you're half starved. Come on, the mess is this way," she turned and led him towards the mess. They arrived, attracting curious glances. Laura was not often seen without Shiva, Zokar or Trudi, and now she was with the intriguing, tall, dark haired young man with the dark blue eyes and the thin but still strongly handsome face. She ordered him a meal, and he handed it to her, ordered three more and carried them to the table. He started wolfing down the food on the first plate after shoving one of the meals towards her.

"Nothing wrong with your appetite," she smiled, handing him a drink.

"The Greys are idiots. Why starve your cattle?" he said resentfully around a mouthful of food. He finished the first plate, slid it aside and reached over for the second plate as he continued his explanation of the Grey threat.

"The humans on Earth have developed their telepathic abilities for the last four thousand years under the suppression generator, so they have become inordinately powerful psychics. When taken off Earth and away from the influence of the suppression generator, their unfettered mental powers could supply the Greys with much more mental 'food' than a human from any other part of the galaxy could."

He had wolfed down the contents of the second plate and pushed it aside, too, then slowed down to a rapid nibble at the contents of the third plate. Laura had only ever seen Gan and Ghrian devour food so quickly before.

"So, what, they just pretended to be stranded there, so they could prey on us?" Laura looked horrified. For some reason, noticed Dom, the Terrans appeared to find the concept of parasitism particularly repulsive.

"Basically, yes. When the second Grey contingent arrived to rescue the first group, which had crashed on Earth, they were scanning carefully as they approached Earth. They realised that something must have caused the first ship to lose power. In that way they discovered and were able to analyse the suppression generator. Once they had analysed what the suppression generator did, they took a few humans off planet and out into deep space to see how powerful they were when *not* suppressed. They discovered that the Earth humans were much too powerful and dangerous to have the generator turned off, and simply started to covertly harvest them. Taken one by one, they were not dangerous, and provided a marvellous, rich food source. The Greys aren't nasty; they put the humans unharmed back after depleting them. And Earth is in the ideal position: they could sneak in from the Void and harvest humans from Earth without the Galactic Union ever knowing, because of the buffer zone and Sol's position all the way out in the isolated Perseus Arm."

He had been rapidly consuming the contents of the third plate of food as he spoke, but Laura forgave his lack of table manners under the circumstances.

"Wait, how do you know all this?" asked Laura.

"I read what I could from their minds while they had me prisoner. We managed to escape this time because we took them completely by surprise, but I don't think we will be so lucky again. By the time we left their station, they had begun to direct their mental powers at draining both you and me. I don't think we will be much use against them in future. The temporal shifting seems to be the only thing that throws them off our trail, and only you and I together can do that, not the normal Terrans or humans."

He finished the last scrap of food on the third plate, then asked, "What's for dessert?"

Chapter Twelve

The Reingold was heading back towards Earth, quickly because Zokar's scanners had read a large fleet of Greys following them. Shiva seemed nervous, and a few times walked up to Zokar's bridge station and shuffled his feet as though he wanted to ask questions, but changed his mind every time. On the second morning of their journey, Zokar heard the human's footsteps stop behind him yet again, but this time they did not wander away after a few minutes.

"How's it going?" asked Shiva quietly.

"We are outpacing them, but only just," replied Zokar.

Shiva's voice dropped even lower, "You want to tell me why you acted like Dom was your long-lost brother, back there at the space station?"

Zokar was silent for a long time, then replied simply, "No." He had still not turned his face away from his console to look at Shiva.

He half-expected to hear his captain walk away again, but Shiva was still standing behind him, and mused, his voice even and controlled, "You're not usually the trusting type."

Zokar was at a loss for words, then turned finally to meet the enquiring blue eyes, "I am afraid that is my nature." The elf kept his expression carefully neutral.

Shiva's eyes bored into his, and then he said, "I think that's the closest I've ever heard you come to an apology." He turned to leave, but Zokar put out a hand to restrain him, and said, "I will say one thing."

Shiva looked at him again with enquiring eyes, and Zokar said, "Dom is trustworthy."

Shiva looked at him cannily and whispered, "Would you trust him with your life?"

"Yes," said Zokar without hesitation. "I'd even trust him with yours."

Shiva blinked several times, but Zokar saw his shoulders relax slightly. The elf turned back to his console, but felt the captain's hand settle on his shoulder. Shiva leaned over and changed the subject, "Do we have enough coolant left to reach Earth?"

"Now, you ask?" Zokar felt himself growing irritable, as he always did after the conversation had skirted too close for comfort to the subject of emotions.

"Well?" pressed Shiva.

"No. Not since you burdened us with collecting those Galactic Union refugees and their ships."

Shiva ignored the elf's snippiness and nibbled his bottom lip, "Suggestions?"

Zokar trotted out his plans, "We can make it to the titanium pools of Orion, then refuel there. Using our onboard coolant refiner, it will take six and a half days to process enough to refill our tanks. It means an indirect path back to Earth, but that may not be a bad thing. Our pursuers may assume that we will head straight to Earth, and diverting from that expected heading may help us to evade capture."

"Okay. How much processed coolant will we have up our sleeves when we leave the Orion pools?

"Seven hours' worth," said Zokar.

Shiva hissed through his teeth, "That's not much."

"Enough to find a safe haven and process what we pick up from the pools."

Shiva nodded. He gave Zokar a brief pat on the shoulder and turned away. Zokar breathed a sigh of relief, feeling drained.

"Navigation, set a course for the Titanium Pools of Orion," said Shiva out loud.

The Reingold turned slightly and headed for Orion.

Just then, Elesk said worriedly, "Captain, we have an

incoming vessel, from the Core... no, two, no...." she drew in a sharp breath, and said softly, "They're Galactic Union, sir."

"Shit," said Shiva succinctly. He leapt back up to the science console to look over Zokar's shoulder at the readouts on the main science viewer.

"They must have sent a rescue contingent," said Zokar, "The ships we rescued... they must have got off a distress call."

"More likely they told the Empress they had found us and this lot were despatched a week ago, Zokar. They're too far out here to have come in the last few hours."

Elesk said in an odd tone, "Sirs, we have clearer readings, now."

"And?" asked Shiva.

Elesk turned to look at them, her silver elvish eyes round, "Sirs, that's no rescue contingent."

"How many ships?" asked Shiva.

Zokar looked over the scanners and said slowly, "It's the main fleet."

Shiva hit the ship wide alert button.

Klaxons sounded throughout the ship, including in the mess. Dom and Laura jumped up as one and strode towards the bridge, Dom grabbing an apple off the table and munching it as he walked.

On the bridge, Shiva leaned over Zokar's shoulder and whispered "Damn. We're low on power, we have a fleet of Greys on our tail, and now we've got to get past the main fleet. I don't like this."

Zokar raised his eyebrows briefly, "You have a talent for understatement. From the point of view of the Galactic Union's main fleet, we would appear to be leading a huge fleet of Grey ships in from the Void in attack formation. The Union fleet will have every reason to believe that the Reingold is leading the Grey fleet against them."

The Union fleet immediately began to fan out.

Shiva stared at the view screen, "Zokar, is it just me or are they fanning out for battle?"

"They are adopting standard battle formation, sir."

"Yeah, that's what I thought. Slow to half speed," ordered Shiva, "We don't want to run up their front." He walked back to stand beside his central station.

Zokar warned him, "If we slow down, the Grey fleet will catch up with us. We will be within range of their weapons in forty-five seconds."

Shiva nodded at Zokar, then turned as Dom and Laura walked onto the bridge, "Can you two cloak us again?"

"Yes," replied Dom confidently, and took his sister's hand. The two of them focused on creating a slight dephasing of the spatio-temporal fabric around the Reingold, and the big ship suddenly shimmered and disappeared off the scanners of both the Galactic Union and Grey ships. There was a jolt, though, then several more, as the Union ships came within range and fired off at the Reingold's last known position.

"We're taking hits!" exclaimed the young weapons officer.

"Helm, drop us down on the vertical axis out of the battle zone, and make optimum speed back to Orion without spiking our fuel consumption," ordered Shiva.

"Aye sir. We are twenty-five degrees down off the likely battle grid now, sir."

"Maintain monitoring."

Dom walked up beside him, "Captain."

"Yes?"

"Perhaps we should warn the Galactic Union fleet of the parasitic nature of these Greys?" suggested Dom.

Shiva looked up at him incredulously, "What?"

"The Greys are mental parasites. The Galactic Union fleet should be warned. As it is, they are going into battle with an enemy which could completely deplete their mental capacities within moments once they are in range. It will be an unfair battle."

"You seriously want me to protect the Galactic Union fleet?"

"I agree with Dom, Shiva," said Laura.

"Of course you do," grumbled Shiva sarcastically, "I'll keep your vote in mind when the next election for captain comes around."

Laura snapped at him, "I agree with him not because he is my brother, but because the enemy of my enemy is my friend. These Greys are a greater threat to Earth than the Galactic Union will ever be. We cannot let the Greys win this first battle. They could wipe out the main fleet, and then just walk in and take the rest of the Galaxy."

"But they have been our allies until now," protested Shiva.

"No!" said Dom, "Not your allies; to them, you are just fodder. They have been harvesting you. The only interest they have in humanity is to domesticate and harvest it."

"The Union and Grey fleets will keep each other busy. Let's just get out of here," suggested Elesk.

Instead of agreeing with his cousin, Zokar asked, "Shiva?"

Shiva hesitated for a few long moments, then turned to look at Zokar's face. The captain pursed his lips, looked from Zokar to Dom and back, then said abruptly to the communications officer, "Get me the Union ship."

While she was hailing the main ship, Shiva walked over and said under his breath to Zokar, "I don't even want to try to figure out why you were willing to leave those Union survivors to rot and die in the Void, but now you're worrying about the safety of their main fleet, which is looking a hell of a lot like it wants to attack us."

Zokar opened his mouth, wondered what to say, then closed it in relief as the main view screen activated and a harsh voice came out. Shiva turned to watch.

A Union admiral appeared on the screen, looking

harassed, and snapped at Shiva, "Captain of the Reingold, I order you to surrender your vessel immediately!"

"No sir, I will not." Shiva held up a hand as the old man glared and opened his mouth and began to speak again, "But I will warn you-" but then Domhan Keallach stepped up beside Shiva, put a hand on his arm, and spoke for him, "General Habersham?"

"S-sir?" The General's face was a study in amazement.

"The Grey aliens which are approaching you, are very dangerous: they are telepathic parasites: they will suck your minds dry and leave you like dry husks if you do not destroy them. This ability begins in them at around one astronomical unit. You would be very wise not to venture closer than that to any of their ships."

"My Lord, are you a prisoner?" asked the General, incredulously.

"I was, but not now. Shiva Kiran and his crew came out here to rescue me."

"But Lord, we have just watched Shiva Kiran run away from a fight like a dog with his tail tucked between his legs and betray his Grey friends."

The General looked confused as Dom snapped at him, "Use your brain, man. The Greys are no friends to the Terrans, nor to the Union. They kidnapped me and kept me hostage, and they have been investigating our galaxy using the Terrans as guinea pigs as a prelude to invasion."

The General's face cleared, "Then you may go. We will stay and fight this menace."

"I am telling you, you cannot fight them, General!"

"Begging your pardon, Lord. I will not fire on the Reingold, because you are on board. But I have direct orders from the Empress to engage any hostile forces which threaten the Union."

Dom turned to Shiva, "Damn it! The only orders which override mine."

The Reingold crew watched as the Galactic Union

and Grey fleets began exchanging fire.

"Helm, get us out of here," said Shiva, "We can't help, and we need to get back to warn the Earth defences about the Greys. And then we have a parley with the Empress to worry about."

The cloaked Reingold dropped a long way below the battle plane, then powered up and headed at hyperdrive towards Orion's belt. Stray laser fire from Grey ships sheared off several pieces of the Reingold as she slipped away, and Zokar heard Shiva swear quietly.

Far behind them, the battle raged. Zokar watched until his scanners could no longer pick up the individual ships.

He was startled by Shiva's quiet voice in his ear, "You want to tell me why you're acting like your grandmother is on one of those Union ships?"

"I do not like my grandmother," Zokar reminded him, with an ironic smile.

"Don't change the subject. What the hell is going on with you?"

"It's nothing," said the elf, but Shiva did not look happy when he returned to the command chair. Zokar hated lying to him.

Chapter Thirteen

The Reingold bridge was strangely tense and quiet. They travelled on towards Orion, but kept their long-range scanners trained on the battle raging far behind them for as long as they could. The two fleets were two vague clouds of light against the darkness.

"It looks like the Grey fleet is backing off, sir," reported Elesk.

"Confirmed," advised Zokar, "They are breaking off and retreating back to the void." He sat back in his chair, but straightened up quickly when he noticed Shiva watching him.

Shiva glared at Zokar, who had the foreboding feeling that he would be having an in-depth discussion with his captain in the not too distant future. But Shiva looked away and addressed Elsek, "Good. It's hardly unexpected. The Galactic Union fleet outnumbers the Grey fleet, and it's more geared towards battle. The Grey ships might have a longer range, but they're not as heavily armed. And despite their responses to Dom's suggestion earlier, the Union ships have been maintaining a distance of more than one astronomical unit from the Grey ships."

Just then, Zokar heard two thumps from beside him and turned to see that Laura and Dom had both collapsed to the floor, unconscious and exhausted after five straight hours of telepathically shielding the Reingold using the effective but very draining method of temporal dephasing.

"We'll be visible!" exclaimed Zokar, and began scanning, then, "Damn! Union Scouts, three of, and they've locked onto our signal."

"Blow them up! Hard about. Don't let them get

away," snapped Shiva, then called for the medics.

The Reingold lurched and then turned agonisingly slowly to follow the scouts, but even though the weapons officer on the Reingold was highly skilled at his job, and managed to shoot two of the scouts out of space before they escaped, the third scout was more powerful and manoeuvrable, and pulled away quickly.

"Damn it! We've lost him," cursed Shiva.

Zokar watched his scanners carefully, and a few minutes later warned, "Sir," as inevitably, three Galactic Union ships dropped out of hyperdrive around them, then three more, then more. Soon the Reingold was surrounded by Galactic Union vessels, and the face of the Empress Arlene came onto their screens. Her voice was characteristically cold as she informed them, "Captain Kiran, your Grey friends appear to have deserted you. Please give me one good reason why I should not solve all my problems immediately by blowing the Reingold out of space?"

"Permit me, sir," said Zokar to Shiva, and flicked one corner of the viewer over to the Reingold's shuttle bay, showing the Empress the Union ships and refugees.

Shiva turned to the Empress and added, "Also, we have rescued a certain passenger, whom you might find of interest, Your Eminence."

He walked over to where the medics were milling about the slumped forms of Dom and Laura, and cleared a path so that the Empress could see Dom's face.

The Empress was silent for a long time. Then the link was cut.

"What's happening?" asked Shiva, staring at the still forms of the vessels hovering around them.

"I suggest that we will find out shortly," said Zokar softly, staring at Shiva intently.

"You mean-"

"They'll either blow us up, or they won't," said Zokar.

Zokar could have heard a pin drop on the bridge. For

many moments, it was silent, then Arlene's face appeared on the view screen again, 'surrender your prisoners."

"They are not prisoners, they are refugees," snapped Shiva and cut the link.

"Are you mad?" gasped Zokar, "Did you just hang up on the Empress? Have you *met* the woman?"

Shiva shrugged, and said, "You know what? I've had a gutful of your precious Empress. Let's get back to Earth. Helm, start moving slowly, turn and work your way out of this nest of ships and take us to Earth. If the Empress wants to blow us up, I'd rather be doing something when it happens, than just hovering here like sitting ducks."

Slowly, the great ship spun on its axis, then powered cautiously between the Union ships, threading its way back towards the Orion cluster and Earth.

Zokar walked up to the command chair, and put one hand on the arm of the chair, the other on the back, and smiled at Shiva, "How did you know she would not blow us up?"

Shiva shrugged and smiled back, "Sometimes, nobody knows what to do and you just have to take the first step. Besides, we have Dom and seven shiploads of refugees on board. She was never going to fire on us."

Zokar nodded thoughtfully, but added, "If you knew Arlene better, Shiva, you would not be so sure."

Shiva stared at him once again, and the elf realised he had probably said too much. He could swear that he could feel the captain's eyes boring into the back of his head as he turned and headed back to his station.

The Reingold made its way slowly out of the cluster of ships and towards Orion. No fire came from the fleet around them, and the Reingold held its fire.

Near Zokar, the head medic said quietly, "They're both coming around, sir."

Zokar looked over to see Laura sitting in a chair, and Dom standing shakily beside her, "What hit me?" asked Laura.

"Exhaustion, we think, and dealing with the Greys," said Shiva.

"Wouldn't that have affected Dom more?" asked Laura.

"I think anything that affects him, affects you, and vice versa," said Zokar quietly.

"Oh."

When Dom suddenly looked up past Zokar and grinned warmly Zokar turned, puzzled, to see what he was looking at. Dom said, "Oh, hi Mum."

"Darling."

Zokar's eyebrows shot up, and the rest of the crew, including Shiva, looked stunned at the softness in her tone. The Empress was gazing at Dom, and then turned to Laura and said, "Laura, it appears that we have much to discuss."

Shiva gave Zokar a look, and Zokar waved him down. *Not now*, Zokar thought frantically, and the human must have read the words in his face, for he said nothing.

The Empress looked back at Dom. "You are much thinner than when I last saw you."

Dom shrugged and gave her an apologetic smile, "Laura's been looking after me, feeding me up since I got on board."

Laura said sadly, "We saved what we could of the original pursuit fleet, ma'am. They're in the cargo hold."

Shiva had insisted they rescue every last one of the Galactic Union crew of the vessels that had escaped, rather than leave them to die slowly in the void when they ran out of fuel. Most of the vessels were small fighters or scouts which had exhausted their energy reserves in the unexpected ferocity of the initial battle with the Greys in the void. The refugees were sullenly grateful, as prisoners of war are wont to be when the alternative is death in the vacuum of space, which entails at best slowly freezing or starving to death in a disabled and drifting vessel.

On the Reingold's main view screen, a tall figure stepped out of the shadows and moved up to stand beside

Arlene, and said something to her.

Shiva was staring at the tall figure, and Zokar felt relief overwhelm him.

"Hello Zokar," said the tall elf.

"Hello, sir," replied Zokar. He did not have to look to see that every eye on the bridge had turned incredulously to look at him.

"I am pleased to see that you are alive and well," added the tall elf beside Arlene.

"And I, you."

"Your father has been concerned for your safety, Zokar," said Arlene.

Once more in the space of five minutes, you could have dropped a pin on the bridge of the Reingold, and it would have echoed resoundingly. The whole bridge crew, including Shiva, fell silent then turned as one to stare at Zokar, then back at the tall figure of Ataar Rizian. The family resemblance between himself and his father, Zokar knew, was uncanny. The only person on the Reingold not looking with amazement at Zokar, he noted, was Elesk.

Shiva looked sideways at Laura, then at Zokar, and screwed up his face and asked Zokar, "That's your *father*?"

"Well, yes of course, sir," answered Zokar quietly.

Laura stared at Zokar.

Chapter Fourteen

Later, in their quarters, Shiva was tearing strips off Zokar, who stood with his head bent.

"You are the son of the consort of the Galactic Empress and you never saw fit to *mention* this to me?"

"It would not have been wise to let it be public knowledge."

"Yes but this is *me*, Zokar, you could have told *me*. I thought you trusted me." Shiva turned away from him in disgust.

Laura, who had been staring at Zokar since they left the bridge, said quietly, "Shiva..."

Zokar stopped her, "It's all right, Laura. Shiva, we are surrounded by telepaths, and you are human. I am an elf: very few can read me. But how long do you think the knowledge would have stayed locked up in your mind, no matter how silent you were about it?"

"Zokar," protested Laura, "You don't understand. Shiva's not a telepath. Even I cannot read him. Your secret would have been safe."

"How was I to know that of all the humans, he would be so different?" demanded Zokar, then turned to Shiva, "I assumed that sharing the information with you would put you in danger."

"Danger? What danger?"

"If it became public knowledge that I were related to the Royal family, not only I but all those around me, would have been subject to the attentions of kidnappers, bounty hunters, terrorists; you name it."

Shiva stared at him incredulously, "But everyone

knows we are associated with Laura now. I'm in that sort of danger anyway. You could have told me any time after I met her. And we're at war with the Galactic Union, now: did that not occur to you?"

"That is true. In my defence, all I can say is that old habits die hard," sighed Zokar. He stared at his feet.

Shiva stared at him thoughtfully, "Or, you might have decided that I would doubt your loyalty to Laura."

Zokar looked up at him blankly for a few seconds before realising what he meant, "And my loyalty to you? Do you doubt that?"

Shiva looked too angry to care. "You could have gone to the Core last year to parley with your father and his wife. You did escape remarkably easily."

"Easily?" Zokar's mind flashed back to the struggle he had escaping the Core, the number of times he had been shot at, or fled crawling through a muddy, parasite-infested ditch on some alien planet, and all to rescue Shiva. "You are in no danger with Laura around. She would detect any such plots and ream the minds of the potential perpetrators. I am merely an elf. I cannot read a mind, let alone control one. The only way I could protect you was with my silence."

"What about when you found out the Empress was going to hunt me down and destroy my ship?"

"I am with you on that very ship, am I not?" asked Zokar, feeling a little lost.

Laura spoke up, "And so am I. Arlene could not have destroyed the Reingold, not with me on board, no matter how much she might have wished to at first," She was still staring at Zokar, and still had the odd look on her face.

"Stop that," Zokar told her.

She looked away, and stopped reading his mind. She was one of very few who could read an elvish mind, but still it was hard work for her, and she had seen enough anyway.

"So why tell everyone now?" demanded Shiva.

"I did not. Arlene did."

"He's right, she's the one that let the cat out of the

bag, not Zokar," said Laura. They both turned to her with puzzled frowns.

"Cat?" asked Zokar.

"Bag?" said Shiva, "Why would you-? Oh, never mind." He rounded on Zokar again, "You should have told me, Zokar."

The elf hung his head, then when Shiva did not say anything more, left the cabin without a word, and without waiting to be dismissed.

Laura looked at Shiva and shook her head.

"What?" growled Shiva.

"I can read his mind, you know."

"So?"

"Don't you want to know what's in it?"

"Bad enough that you invade his privacy. I don't want your hearsay."

"You are upset."

"You could say that."

"Shiva, please don't be hard on Zokar."

"Hard on him? That conniving old bastard?"

"You need to cool down."

"I thought I knew where I stood with him. Of all people, he's the one I thought I could trust," he spat on the ground, "And now, it turns out he's just like the rest; secrets and lies."

"One secret he kept from you, and that was to protect you!" she protested.

"It was a pretty major one, wouldn't you say?" Shiva growled.

"Which is why it needed to be kept from you. Damn it, Shiva, he's my brother, apparently. And I'm not with you on this one. I'm going to talk to him."

"Step brother," corrected Shiva grumpily, "Go then, but don't be too long."

He paced his cabin angrily, and stood on Gan's tail. Gan meowed squawkily, stood up archly and walked out, then strolled off behind Laura.

The elf looked up from the sofa in his cabin, as first Laura walked in then Gan, who stalked in and sat at Zokar's feet.

"What's he doing here?" Zokar asked quietly, indicating Gan.

"Perhaps he's just as pissed off with his master as I am," suggested Laura wryly, "I am sorry for his behaviour, Zokar," she sat down beside Zokar and put a comforting hand on his.

Zokar stared at her, and asked, "Do you know how long it is, since anyone apologised to me because they thought my *feelings* were hurt?" His lips curled in a wry smile.

She laughed, and said, "I can see the irony in that, I must admit."

He chuckled, but she was still watching him with that oddly penetrating stare of hers which sometimes unnerved even Zokar.

"What are you going to do?" she asked, patting his hand.

"There's nothing I can do. He believes me, or he doesn't." The elf's mouth thinned into a grim line.

"I believe you," said Laura.

"Ah, the surety of a telepath. What luxuries you have in your life. Shiva does not have that. Nor do I. We always live in doubt of others."

"Believe it or not, I do know what that's like, Zokar. I was raised on Earth, remember, before the suppression generator was destroyed. I know what it's like to live in doubt, always alone in one's own thoughts."

Zokar looked down and sat there miserably. Laura was silent for a few moments, then asked, "Before Trudi and I came along, you two only had each other, didn't you?"

"Yes," he said quietly.

"If it's any consolation, I don't have to read his mind

to know that he loves you, like a brother."

Zokar hung his head and did not reply. There was no answer in an elvish mind to that statement.

She patted his hand, stood up and left his cabin.

Zokar looked at Gan and Ghrian, now both lying at his feet purring. He growled at Gan, "Go back to your master."

Gan looked up at him, looked out the door, then stood up and leaned against Zokar, purring, then sat back down at his feet, finally curling up and going to sleep next to his littermate.

It was hours later that Shiva turned up.

The elf stood stiffly to attention, "Captain."

"Zokar. I lost my cat."

"He's here."

"I can see that."

Shiva looked for long minutes at Zokar, "Zokar. What I said-"

"Was in error. You are forgiven. Take your cat and go."

Shiva turned on his heel and left the cabin, and Zokar sat down, shaking his head. He looked at Gan, then said, "Go, then."

The big cat stood up and trotted out the door after its master.

Zokar went to find Trudi. He found her alone in the science lab and buried his face in her long dark hair.

"What's wrong, baby?" she asked softly, turning around to take him in her arms.

"Humans," he grumbled, and she chuckled, "Don't kid yourself, you love us."

"I wish I had never met a human."

Chapter Fifteen

The Titanium pools of Orion were a source of liquid titanium, which lay in calm pools on the intensely hot surface of five asteroids which had been pulled into orbit around one of the moons of a hot inner planet in one of the multitude of star systems in the Orion cluster. Gaseous titanium was one of the main coolants used in the hyperdrive core on the Reingold, and the fuel which was used fastest in the operation of the drive. They had to replace it frequently as it became saturated with by-products from the wormhole. It was contained in magnetic bottles when not in use. To collect the metal from the pools, shuttles would approach the pools, their battle shields protecting them from the intense heat, and use finely balanced magnetic mooring lines and balloons to collect the titanium. All of the ship's complement of shuttles would have to be used, in order to collect the fuel quickly and get away before they were detected by any Grey vessels.

Shiva was irritable and nervous. Even though this was routine work for the Reingold's crew, they were performing it under battle conditions. The Greys probably knew of this refuelling point, and could decide to check it at any minute. Zokar came up to the command chair, and handed him an estimate.

"Six hours?" fretted Shiva, and commented fretfully, "That's an *eternity*, Zokar."

"We can do nothing else. To leave here with less than a full tank of fuel would be risky. We do not know what we will find when we arrive at Earth, or encounter on the way there."

"I know, I know," said Shiva.

Zokar hesitated, then put a brief hand on Shiva's shoulder before turning and stepping back up to his station. Laura, standing beside Shiva, noticed and smiled quietly to Zokar as he walked past her.

The shuttles deployed. Laura regarded the view screen intently, and so did Shiva. The sleek shuttles began to ferry titanium, each shuttle trailing behind it on the return trip from the asteroids a huge blob of liquid metal which swirled and flowed within the invisible magnetic bottle. The trip down to the asteroid was quick, the one back painfully slow. Too great a change in velocity or direction, and the vast balloon of liquid titanium could pop and disgorge itself into the vacuum of space, its intense heat vaporising any shuttle which it happened to touch. When each returning shuttle managed to manoeuvre into the vast cargo hold of the Reingold, it had to line up with the magnetic collector using sensors to detect it, and wait to empty its load before switching off the bottle and returning to the asteroid. That was the slowest part of the trip, and a line-up of shuttles quickly built up outside the Reingold's cargo bay doors.

Zokar was watching the screen closely and directing shuttles occasionally when they drifted too close to each other. He glanced at the captain's chair, and noticed that Laura looked a little pale. Dom suddenly turned up on the bridge looking nervous, and asked, "Did anyone else feel that?" Zokar turned to ask, "Feel what?" but then the ship's alert siren sounded yet again.

"Incoming!" called Elesk, "Twenty-one vessels, attack formation!"

"Those are Grey ships!"

Shiva swore, and slammed the communications button himself, "Shuttle commanders, we are under attack! Ditch your loads and dock NOW!"

It was hopeless, Zokar knew. Even if they ditched their loads, the shuttles could not all make it inside the Reingold before the Grey ships reached firing range.

Pools of titanium swam haphazardly around the shuttles and the Reingold as the shuttles struggled to comply.

"Laura, Dom, do something!" yelled Shiva, and Dom raced over to his sister and grabbed her hand. They both shut their eyes and squinted as though someone had thrown water in their faces, then stood staring at the Grey ships on the view screen. After a few seconds, Dom groaned, and called to Shiva "It's not working, They're already too close! They're just soaking up our energy as we throw it at them."

"Try helping the shuttles then!" suggested Shiva, and the twins turned their attention to the shuttles. Suddenly, the titanium that was drifting through space around the shuttles gathered into a coherent blob and flung itself towards the Grey ships, spreading rapidly into a white vapour which obscured the Greys" view of the Reingold and the shuttles. With the titanium cleared away from between the Reingold and the shuttles, the shuttles were suddenly free to be sucked in to the Reingold's hold at dizzying speed, one by one.

Shiva waited until the last shuttle was in, then slammed the communications button again, "Close cargo bay doors!"

The doors started their excruciatingly slow closing sequence, and Shiva turned to Laura and Dom again, "Can you-"

"Sure," said Laura, and suddenly the great ship boomed as the bay doors shut almost instantly.

Meanwhile, Zokar had been busy snapping orders into the intercom, "Ready for hyperdrive.... now, sir!"

"Go!" said Shiva to the helmsman, and the Reingold shot into hyperdrive.

"Those Greys," grumbled Laura groggily, "They're hard enough to fight at a distance."

"And impossible up close," added Dom, "They just suck the power out of you."

Shiva looked at them both, "Are you going to be okay?"

"Fine," said Laura, "Just keep us away from any Grey

ships, hey, Shiva."

He nodded, looking worried, then turned to Zokar, "Casualties?"

"None, sir," said the elf, looking mildly surprised.

But Shiva was worrying his bottom lip with his teeth, and Laura asked him, "What?"

"Why are they back? Why are they chasing us?" asked Shiva.

"I think they're trying to stop us from warning Earth," suggested Laura.

"Or the Union. They may not realise that we have already warned the Union," agreed Shiva.

Shiva nodded, and started to speak, but Zokar beat him to it, "I think we got enough fuel on board to get to Earth. I'll get you a summary in about ten minutes."

"Good, thanks," said Shiva as Zokar left for the cargo hold and engine rooms.

Chapter Sixteen

Zokar sat working quietly at his station on the bridge, feeling out of sorts. Shiva was sitting in the central chair, looking glum and thoughtful. He turned his face to Zokar, and Zokar thought that if he was some kind of lowly bait worm, the captain would have given him a similar look. But then Shiva surprised him by standing and walking over to Zokar's station.

Shiva put a hand on the back of Zokar's chair and murmured, "I think we should team up with the Empress."

Zokar stared at him. It was the last thing he had expected of the human, but he sat back in his chair and asked, "Why?"

"Remember what I said to you, Zokar, about how sometimes, nobody knows what to do and you just have to take the first step?"

"Yes."

"Well, maybe this is one of those times. The Empress is too proud, Laura is too scared, because don't forget she's new to all this, and feels responsible for protecting Earth, and you? You won't go against me. Your father won't go against the Empress, so he's waiting for her decision. Dom, well he's a bloodhound, alright, but he's not really a strategist. All he has ever known is the hunt for his sister."

Zokar nodded, and asked, "And you think an alliance is necessary because?"

"Two reasons, Zokar. Because, one; an alliance always beats a war. Two; I have a gut feeling these Greys might be a bigger threat than anyone has realised."

"Hmmm. Yes, they have managed to navigate the

void across from Andromeda. That speaks of a highly developed technology."

"Yeah, and everyone's been looking at their weaponry technology and saying that it's not very advanced, but the thing is, they don't need it to be advanced, Zokar. If they can suck your brains dry before you can aim your guns, why would they need bigger guns?"

"How can I help?"

"Well, you wouldn't have been worrying yourself sick for three days about your father unless there was some genuine affection there. If we have family connections we might as well use them."

"We?"

"We."

Zokar looked down, "Aye, sir."

"Come on, let's get this over with," said Shiva, and they walked down to the command chair.

Shiva stood up straight, and whispered to Zokar, "Do you ever wish you looked more... military?"

Zokar stared down at Shiva's golden hair and blue eyes, a slightly mocking smile curling about his lips.

Shiva looked up at him and sighed, "No, I guess *you* don't."

Out loud, he called to Elesk, "Direct communications to Empress Keallach, Elesk."

"Aye, sir," her eyes and hands flew over the board, and then she said, "Communication established, sir."

The elegant face of the Empress Arlene was suddenly on the view screen, and Shiva was glowering at her. Zokar could understand Shiva's reaction. Arlene's attitude and demeanour were beyond condescending towards the young captain. She was looking at Shiva now like he was something she had stepped in and was considering scraping off her foot.

"Empress," said Shiva tightly.

"Captain Kiran," her eyes were cool, speculative, but Zokar noticed that she glanced at him with a quick look of acknowledgement before fixing her gaze back on Shiva.

"Ma'am, I believe that you and I are in a unique position to commence discussion about a military alliance between our two empires."

She stared at him for a long time, then her eyes showed some interest, and she said, "Really? You surprise me, Captain Kiran."

"Why is that, Ma'am?"

"I would not have picked you for a diplomat. A mindless military drone, but not a diplomat."

"Ignore the insult," muttered Zokar as quickly as he could. Shiva grimaced and replied slowly, "Perhaps given the circumstances under which we have met to date, Ma'am, that is understandable. But I believe there is a greater good here, which needs to be addressed: the good of the civilian population of this galaxy."

"So speaks the man who assisted my daughter to obliterate my entire fleet a year ago."

"Ma'am, I understand –"

"No you do not," she snarled at him, "To you they were just numbers, but to me; understand that my soldiers were the bravest and most capable of my friends. I had many friends in the military." Zokar kept his face impassive.

Shiva was silent. Zokar spoke up when he realised his captain had no answer for the Empress. He said quietly, "Arlene, that is the past, and nothing we can do now will change what has happened. Perhaps though, we can act now to prevent another such occurrence in the future?"

She regarded him silently for a long time, then whispered quietly, "So like your father."

Then she cut the link.

Shiva looked surprised, "Why did she do that?"

"She required time to consider your offer," said Zokar.

"I hardly had a chance to elaborate on it."

"She is not stupid. You offered an alliance, and she will consider that. I think that it went rather well."

"Okay, Zokar, whatever you say. I think it sucked."

"At least she thinks you look military," smiled Zokar.

Shiva shook his head, "You have a strange sense of humour."

"Yes," agreed the elf, "So now what?"

"We wait, I suppose. There is nothing more to be done. We head for Earth and wait for a response from Arlene," he sighed, then looked at the elf, "Can we trust her, Zokar?"

"What do you mean?" asked Zokar.

"I mean, what if she agrees to an alliance, then destroys our fleet and the Greys?"

Zokar pursed his lips, "I do not know."

"I wouldn't put it past her," said Shiva.

"Nor would I," sighed Zokar.

Chapter Seventeen

The Reingold made way for Earth. Laura and Dom had recovered and helped wherever they could, hiding the ship from Union patrols and boosting the power systems. At the moment they were both on the bridge, making the junior crew nervous and irritating Zokar by floating small objects around the bridge.

Zokar knew the names of the solar system planets now. They came in past tiny, frozen Pluto and were now approaching the blue ball of Neptune, and the scanners were already picking up the Terran fleet. Like a blue asteroid belt the blue ships lay in a protective ring around the inner planets, just outside Saturn's orbit. The two giants of the Solar system, Jupiter and Saturn, lay inside the protective ring, as did the smaller planets of Mars, Earth, Venus and Mercury.

"Why are they patrolling out so far?" asked Trudi, who was sitting next to Zokar.

"It's system protection," answered Shiva from behind them.

Zokar noticed her confused look and explained, "If you disturb the orbits or even destroy one or more of the bigger planets in a system, that destabilises the whole star system and can devastate an inner planet just as effectively as blowing it up," Zokar told her, "To protect Earth, you have to protect the whole system."

"What about the smaller outer planets?"

"Immaterial," answered Shiva just as briefly as earlier.

Zokar shot him a curious look, then explained, "Yes,

they are too small and outside the orbits of the giants, so provide very little gravitational influence on the system as a whole."

"So, what, the outer planets are expendable?"

"Yes," confirmed Zokar, "At least, so far as protecting the population of Terra itself is concerned."

"Ah," said Trudi, and looked with regretful eyes at the beautiful blue globe of Neptune still before them, gradually moving across the view screen as they passed the austere planet.

"What are they doing?" asked Laura, as the thousands of ships in the belt turned to the Reingold and began to flash the huge vessel with their landing lights.

Shiva was silent, and Zokar said quietly, "They are welcoming us back."

They watched as every vessel in the flotilla turned and pulsed their unbearably bright landing lights at the Reingold, once, twice, three times, then turned slowly back to their position facing outwards, facing the potential threat from the Galactic Union. Within the space between Earth and the ring of vessels, the thin lights of supply ships moving back and forth constantly were just visible.

"How long can your people keep up this battle?" Shiva asked Laura, looking up at the much thinner hemisphere of ships above them, all flashing their lights too.

"Forever," answered Laura with an odd note in her voice.

Shiva stared at her and she explained, "We're Terrans."

"They are born fighters, Shiva," observed Zokar.

"Natural born killers," agreed Trudi absently, and the whole bridge crew turned to stare at the human woman. She looked down at them, "What?" Dom looked at her with an odd expression in his dark eyes.

"And you're the sweet, shy one," smiled Zokar.

"Why isn't it a globe?" asked Trudi suddenly, waving at the flat ring of ships in the elliptical plane of Sol's solar system, "Why is it just a ring? I thought you people thought in three dimensions?"

"Logistics," explained Zokar patiently, "It would not be fuel efficient to leave the galactic plane and attack the system from so far above. You would double your fuel requirements in getting here, especially so far out on the Rim. Also, the dense background of stars on the galactic plane makes an attacking ship far more difficult to detect. All things considered, the most likely direction of attack is along that plane."

"So if your solar system did not align with the galactic plane, you would align the axis of the ring of ships with the galactic plane rather than the system's orbital plane?" asked Trudi.

"And," Zokar observed proudly, "… natural born strategists." Impulsively, he leaned across and planted an approving kiss on the top of Trudi's head, and found the discomfort of the junior crew around them amusing enough to consider repeating the action on a regular basis. Zokar noticed Shiva give him and Trudi a quick grin, but the captain said nothing.

Trudi contented herself with gazing at Neptune. She was still relatively new to space travel, Zokar remembered, and seemed transfixed by the mysterious, cold beauty of the perfect blue globe. He followed her gaze and frowned as he noticed something odd. Zokar leaned forward and increased the magnification on the viewer Trudi was watching. Trudi asked him curiously, "Neptune doesn't have an atmosphere, does it?"

"No," said Laura from behind them.

"Then what's that grey area around the planet?" asked Trudi.

There was silence for a second, then Shiva swore, and Zokar clipped, "Scanning!"

They looked on in horror as the scanner picked up the image and magnified it.

Shiva exclaimed, "My God, Zokar, that's - damn it!

That's not around the planet, that's behind it! They're coming in using the planet as cover. Communications, warn the System defences."

"Elesk to Terran defences, you have a large fleet, incoming hostiles, warning, this is a red alert, you have a large fleet, incoming hostiles, coming in from behind... what's that planet called?"

"Neptune," supplied Trudi, and Elesk continued, "-Neptune."

The Reingold turned to face the menace, and Zokar said, "Shiva, this is not a good idea, Laura and Dom cannot protect us against Greys, remember?

Elesk broke in in a worried tone of voice, "Sir, there is no response from System defences. I think our communications are being scrambled or drained of power."

"But they're all still watching us, right?" asked Shiva, "Helm, keep turning, and start firing!"

"We're hopelessly out of range, sir!" protested the helmsman.

"Don't you think I know that?" snarled Shiva, and reached forward and hit the weapons button himself, scraping his hand expertly across the board so that the Reingold released a barrage of fire straight towards Neptune.

Back on the blue ships further in towards Earth, the commanders started paying attention, "What are they doing?"

"Are there hostiles out there?"

"Hail the Reingold," said a few commanders.

"No response. Sir! It appears our communications are out!"

"Battle stations!" and the battle claxons started sounding on the blue ships, a contingent of which surged forwards to flank the Reingold and see past Neptune.

"Holy shit!" whispered one commander.

"Hell," said another.

"Wait a minute, they're Greys."

"Then why is the Reingold firing on friendlies?"
"Has the Reingold been hijacked?"

Chapter Eighteen

On the Reingold bridge, Dom was tugging Laura by the hand, an idea forming in his head, "Come with me!"

"Dom, what are you doing?" asked Laura.

"We can't help if we get any closer to the Greys," he said as he tugged her through the ship, and pushed her into a shuttle, then hit the emergency battle jettison button, and the tiny shuttle shot out behind the Reingold, back toward the main Terran fleet and Earth.

"Are you mad? This thing doesn't have the range to even get us back to the Terran fleet, let alone Earth!" she railed at him.

"I don't think that's going to be a problem," said Dom, indicating the Terran ships rapidly closing on the shuttle's position, "The Terran fleet is coming to us."

"What are you going to do?"

"Keep us away from the Greys, and warn the Terrans. Communications are out, remember, and as far as they're concerned, the Greys are friendlies. We need to warn Earth."

"Since when did you give a damn about Earth?" she looked askance at him, and he realized she was probably remembering their last big argument, when Dom had wanted Laura to leave Earth to its fate and serve the Galactic Union.

"Since you lot all turned up and rescued me. I'm starting to like the Terran way of thinking."

She leaned back and looked at him, then chuckled.

Just then the shuttle was rocked by a sudden turbulence, and Laura righted it, a little too fast for Dom, who felt a wave of nausea come over him.

"What was that?"

"Scanning," she said, working the awkward, unfamiliar controls of the shuttle's view screen, "Oh, no."

"What?" he demanded, then looked up at the screen, "Oh, shit."

To the left and above them, a swarm of Galactic Union vessels were approaching the Terran fleet, and the Terrans had broken off to turn and fight them.

"No, no, no!" shouted Dom at the view screen, and Laura said, "Damn it, the Terrans are fighting the wrong damned battle!"

"And doing it too well," observed Dom, as they watched the Terran ships turn on the Galactic Union vessels and start to pick them off in savage dogfights.

Chapter Nineteen

Back on the Reingold, Shiva watched the rear scanners as the Terrans began to fight the Galactic Union ships.

"They haven't fired back," he said hopefully.

"Yes, and your natural born killers haven't bloody noticed that fact," said Zokar angrily.

"The Terrans are slaughtering them," observed Shiva.

"Fight back," whispered Zokar, and Shiva glared at him.

"I don't think it will take Arlene long to figure that out, Zokar. She's not going to let her fleet be destroyed."

"What can we do?" asked Zokar, "They're all ignoring us."

"Let's make them take notice," said Shiva. "Helm, hard about. Take us above the Galactic Union Fleet, well up off the plane of the galaxy, and behind them. Then I want to come in from behind them, but firing upwards, not hitting anything."

The great ship lurched, and they all held on as the hard turn challenged the artificial gravity on the huge vessel.

On the Empress's vessel, Ataar Rizian asked, "What's the Reingold doing?" as the huge vessel turned hard and sped up behind them.

"Who cares?" answered Arlene tightly, "We have to fight back, Ataar."

"But how? We can't tell the fleet what to do, because we have no communications."

"Start firing on my command. Once the command ship starts firing, the rest of the Generals will follow suit. We can't just sit here and be picked off, we'll-"

Her words were drowned out in a groaning howl from the gravity compensators on the battle cruiser, and the Reingold almost clipped the Empress's ship as it closed from behind, then flew overhead, firing a barrage of destructive beams up into the space above their heads. The Empress cringed, ducking instinctively down as the great old ship groaned past them, too close and too soon out of hyperdrive for comfort, then turned in a tight arc to head back out towards Neptune.

"Damn you, Shiva Kiran!" cried the Empress, then froze, and asked, "But why didn't he vaporize us? And what the hell is he firing at?"

"Nothing!" roared Ataar triumphantly, and leapt to the weapons console, "Parallel him!" he yelled to the helmsman, "Fly with him!"

"Ataar, what are you doing?" demanded Arlene, but Ataar noticed that she did not countermand his order, and he smiled to himself.

Not trusting anyone else to comprehend quickly enough what he was doing, Ataar aimed their weapons high, making sure they would miss the Reingold, and the two ships joined in swooping around in a tight arc between the Earth and Galactic Union fleets, firing harmlessly above their heads.

On one of the blue ships, Admiral Mick McCosker said, "What the hell are they doing? Shooting into the air?"

"Should we return their fire, sir?" asked Nick doubtfully.

"What fire, son?" asked McCosker, who now looked younger than Nick, but still called him son, "I mean, they're not firing at us, but they're not hitting the Union fleet either. They've gone straight past them."

"Then what –"

"It's a signal! I'll bet their communications are out,

just like ours!"

"But the Empress's ship is with them."

"It is," said McCosker, steepling his fingers, then made a quick decision, "Join them."

"What?"

"You heard me. Do it!"

A sleek blue ship from the front of the Terran fleet suddenly accelerated and came quickly up alongside the Reingold.

"It's working," said Shiva breathlessly to Zokar. Zokar shook his head, "Brilliant."

The three lead ships hammered towards the Grey fleet, and after some initial confusion, the Terran and Galactic Union fleets rallied and came along behind them, the Galactic Union ships having to do a quick about face to do so.

The Greys came face to face with a united front of Galactic Union and Earth ships.

The fleets slowed and fanned out, as the two lines of vessels faced each other, jockeying to maintain themselves out of firing range... then a single shot came out from a Grey vessel and disintegrated a blue Terran vessel in one hit.

"Bastards!" exclaimed Nick. "The Greys have swapped sides! Hell, everyone has, even the Union ships! General, what in God's name is going on?"

"I don't know, son," said McCosker, "But look alert, it could change again, you never know."

Nick raised his eyebrows and returned his attentions to his console, "We need communications," he growled, and fiddled anxiously with the console.

"You won't get it," guessed McCosker, "I'd say the Greys are creating that interference."

"It just doesn't seem right, shooting on the Greys."

"Son, they just vaporised an Earth vessel. Besides, Zokar Rizian and Shiva Kiran are on the Reingold. Do you feel like second-guessing those two and playing our own strategy?"

"No, I'd just feel better if we could talk to somebody."

"Yeah."

"That's a big fleet," commented Nick, in a suddenly hushed tone, as they swung to come into full view of the Grey fleet.

McCosker looked at him, and looked at the pale faces of the young crew members around him. He flicked a button on his chair arm, and suddenly they were seeing behind them, an excellent view of the united Galactic Union and Terran fleets, "Not too damned shabby ourselves, son."

Chapter Twenty

On board the Reingold, Zokar waited silently for the battle to reach them. The battle began in eerie silence, a ballet of moving ships, a silent fireworks display, strangely beautiful, yet unsettling, until explosions were heard as a disruptor barrage struck the Reingold, and Zokar felt the impact shudder the giant ship and heard the distant screams of his shipmates, the tearing of metal, the hissing of precious air escaping, the smell of burning plastic, and the repeated clunking down of airlock doors as sections of the ship and their occupants were brutally cut off from the sections that still had oxygen and an intact hull.

Shiva and Zokar called out such rapid fire orders that the bridge staff struggled to keep up with the barrage of commands, but the captain and the elf were all over the bridge, slapping buttons here, working controls there, and helping the junior staff wherever they could. The Reingold groaned as it turned and fired upon the Grey ships at long range, the turns required in battle too fast for the giant old bulk tanker.

"Keep firing! Don't let them get close!" yelled Shiva, "Hold your formation, dammit, helm, we mustn't block the Union ships' fire! We need to hold those Greys back!"

The big ship floundered, but suddenly Zokar reported, "We have an escort."

A small contingent of blue ships had gathered around the Reingold, and began to fire off salvos at the Grey ships attacking the big vessel. Soon the Reingold had fallen back behind the battle lines, because she was after all, only a tanker, and the faster Opal ships and Union battle cruisers carried the battle lines quickly back out past Neptune.

Zokar said, "Enough, Shiva, that's enough. We've done our bit. We've warned Earth. Let the battleships take it from here."

Shiva stared at him blankly for a few moments, then looked intently out at the fleet, a long way from them now. The Reingold still had its escort of blue Opal ships, but could be no real use to the Earth defences and would probably only be in the way.

"We have wounded," said Trudi softly to the two of them.

Shiva finally nodded, and said quietly, "Helm, make for Earth orbit. Trudi, can you organise triage and help medical?"

"Yes," she said, and hurried from the bridge.

Zokar stepped down to the central chair, tore a strip off his own tunic sleeve, and took Shiva's hand in his.

"What?" asked Shiva, then fell silent as he realised that he had gashed his hand badly when the Reingold was hit and he had been slammed across the torn edge of a console. He sat quietly as Zokar wrapped his hand firmly in the cloth and tied it off.

"Thanks," he muttered, as Zokar finished, then asked, "Are you alright?"

"Fine. I will check the rest of the bridge crew."

Shiva hit the central console button and said, "Damage control reports to the Captain immediately please. Medical is working and triage in place. If you can't get there, contact the bridge and medics will shuttle around to your position."

Then Shiva suddenly looked around and asked, "Where's Laura?"

Zokar shrugged, "She's okay. She was with Dom."

The Reingold limped back to Earth, pitted and scarred, like a huge guard dog limping back torn and bleeding to its home after seeing off the local curs. Shiva's face was grim. The big vessel was going to need major repairs. He could feel it in the sluggishness of her helm response, hear it in the still howling pressure loss alarms from the depths of his ship.

Suddenly communications returned. The blue ships escorting the Reingold contacted them.

Nick, Ryan and Karl smiled at Zokar, and McCosker's voice said, "Hey, Zokar, old buddy! How are you going?"

"It appears that I owe you my thanks yet again," said Zokar, warmly.

"Don't mention it sonny," grinned McCosker. Zokar flinched.

"General, do you have shuttles available? Can you scan the Reingold for isolated crew and get shuttles to assist them?" asked Shiva.

The General looked at Shiva, and said, "Sure, Captain. We can do that."

The Opal ships began to swing around the Reingold, and shuttles nestled against the great ship's hull, setting out force field nets, like glowing blue spider webs against the outside of the Reingold's hull, to hold the atmosphere in each section as they entered through the airlocks and began to retrieve injured and isolated crew members.

Chapter Twenty-one

As the Reingold struggled into Earth orbit for yet another bout of repairs, the battle raged on from just outside Saturn's rings, around the small round globe of Uranus, and towards the frozen blue planet Neptune.

On board the flagship of the Galactic Union fleet, Arlene watched the battle with great interest. After the initial confusion, the Union and Terran forces were working together, surprisingly well. "These Terrans do tactics like it's second nature," she said, as a group of Opal ships flanked the Greys and drove them into a pincer grip between themselves and a line of Union ships, so that the Union ships could hammer them relentlessly with disruptor fire.

"Are you thinking what I'm thinking?" asked Ataar, his hand on the back of her chair.

"I'm thinking, I'm glad they're on our side," she murmured, not wanting the crew to hear.

"Exactly," agreed Ataar, "I think I'm glad we didn't end up going to war with Earth. I think we would have lost."

She turned to raise both eyebrows at him, then turned her attention back to the battle, which was going much better now that they had communications back. One of the bigger Grey ships had been disabled, and it must have been the one that had the jamming equipment on it, because they had communications now, throughout the fleet.

What worried Arlene was the feeling that perhaps Ataar was correct. Despite the fact that Earth was a tiny, insignificant planet on the edge of one of her galaxies, the Terrans now controlled a sizeable chunk of that galaxy and had engineered an alliance with the Galactic Union and the

Fey. In the eighteen short months since they had been freed from their long captivity, the Terrans had shown themselves to be a force to be reckoned with. They now appeared to have control of two of her children, and the loyalty of her consort's son. She was starting to suspect that Ataar was beginning to like them, too. What was it, she wondered a little irritably, about these damned Terrans? Why did she find herself in the thick of a damned war on the edge of their system, defending their insignificant little star and their tiny water planet, fighting for her life against an enemy, the Greys, to whom she had hardly given a moment's thought until today?

She sighed and concentrated on the clear and present danger of the Grey ships around them, and hoped that nothing else would go wrong this day.

Chapter Twenty-two

Laura was cursing Dom, "What the Hell did you think you were doing, getting us stuck out here in a shuttle in the middle of a battle?"

"Will you stop yelling at me?" he growled back.

"Why? Why the hell shouldn't I yell at you? I should be helping with the fight, not stuck out here in this-" she kicked the shuttle's wall, "- bus!"

"Calm down! We have communications back, we can call for help," he shifted the controls and aimed the shuttle back towards Saturn, which suddenly seemed a long, long way away.

"And who will come, Dom? Who will come? Jesus, you have a real talent for getting me into trouble, you know that?"

He sulked and glared at the controls, then whispered, "Uh-oh."

Laura felt it too, and said, "That's a Grey field. Try temporal shifting us, quick!"

But it was too late, they both fainted dead away as a five Grey ships came out of hyperdrive only metres from them. For many minutes there was silence in the shuttle, then the shuttle swayed and began to move, and was gradually sucked by a tractor beam into the hold of the biggest Grey ship. The ship turned and began to move away, giving a wide berth to the still battling Earth and Union forces and heading back behind the Grey lines.

Chapter Twenty-three

Far away from the conflict near Earth, on the opposite side of the galaxy, was a small gold sun very much like Sol. Near the third moon of the fourth planet around this sun, a ship floated in stationary orbit around the moon.

The ship looked like a giant conical beehive, narrow at the front and fat and rounded at the back end. The surface was dotted with thousands of dark, round holes in neat rows. Chambers within the ship contained a Bug each. The Bugs were like giant wasps, black, winged, with red and yellow patterns on their bodies and wings. Each bug was about five metres long, with a wingspan of over twenty metres.

A Bug landed on the outside of the ship. The bug folded its wings back along its horizontal body, holding a neatly rolled human in its two front legs and walking on the remaining four. It crawled in through a dark hole in the side of the ship, into the corridors within, and headed deeper into the bowels of the vessel with its prize. As it passed other Bugs, it exchanged a faint puff of pheromones with its hive-mates to identify itself. The human in its grasp moaned and twisted slightly, but the Bug ignored it and marched on. Eventually it came to a corridor where the food supply was being stored for the long flight ahead. Worker Bugs were weaving narrow alcoves out from the sides of the huge corridors, and warrior Bugs were bringing humans in to stuff into each alcove. The corridors were narrowed by the lining of dazed humans, so that when the alcoves were completed and stuffed there was barely room for two Bugs to pass each other in the corridors. The Bug waited for the next alcove to be completed, then stuffed its parcel carefully into the alcove feet first. The Bugs working on the alcoves swiftly wove a stiff cover of web over the alcove, muffling the now-distressed cries of the human within.

Rolled and preserved humans formed a large part of the food supply within the depths of the ship, as they did the food supply on all the ships in the Bug fleet. The Bug fleet was about to head for the Core, because something had weakened the defences of the Galactic Union, and now word (or, rather, click) had come through to the Bugs that the entire remaining Galactic Union fleet had headed away, out to the Perseus Arm. The Bugs were on a food-gathering mission, and with them came their bulk carriers, huge vessels into which the Bugs had already stuffed thousands of cocooned and still - barely - living humans obtained en route to their current position. There was a buzz of excitement throughout the ship at the prospect of going to the Core. The planets near the Core were said to be overflowing with juicy humans.

Below them, on the moon's surface, a young boy held his mother's arm and pointed intently skywards at the strange shaped ships appearing in their atmosphere. She dragged him back into the house and lifted the carpet in the far corner of the living room, raising a stiff wooden trapdoor and helping the boy inside. Once inside she brought the door back over and used a string to pull the carpet back into place. There was about three month's supply of food and water in the hidden cellar, and they huddled together silently.

Above them, there was an ominous buzzing, then a scraping sound as a Bug inspected the house. Finding nobody home, it left, with a whoosh and a buzz of wings. The woman peeked out from a periscope in the cellar and when she had seen and heard nothing for hours, took a chance and turned on the communication terminal in the cellar. She and the boy sat and watched in horror as the Bugs decimated their planet like a plague of giant locusts. The Bugs had never ventured in this close to the Core before, but the woman was from a frontier planet on which they were endemic and raided often. She and her son survived. Millions did not.

Eventually, the Bug ships turned and headed for the next system, one step closer to the Core. The woman in the cellar sent out a distress signal to the nearest Galactic Union star base, and the officer carrying the message was grim as he handed the chip to his commanding officer. The commander of the star base hit his communications button straight away, and said, "Get me General Nima at Union Central Command!"

The communications officer hastily complied with the barked orders, and the commanding officer said, "General, we have a problem. How soon can the main fleet deploy out to the Centaurus Arm?"

"They can't," answered General Nima of Union Central, "They're fighting Greys in the outer Perseus Arm."

"What? I knew they were deployed, but what the Hell are they doing out there?"

"It's a long story. The thing is, we only have a skeleton fleet here. What's the problem?" asked the General.

"You're gonna love this. The Bugs are on the move. They're heading for the Core. They just swarmed the Three Moons of Kandahar," said the commander.

"Oh, shit. They've never ventured in that far before," said the General.

"We need help, here."

"I'll get on it. We'll send a strike team, maybe they can harass the Bugs and slow them down."

"I think it's going to take more than a strike team," said the star base commander.

"Well, that's all we have at the moment," said the General, "So that's what you"ll get."

"How many ships can you spare?" asked the commander.

"Fifty."

"It's not a lot. Can you contact the main fleet too?"

"Of course," agreed the General, "I'll let you know

what's happening."
"Thanks."

Chapter Twenty-four

"Exalted One?" ventured Arlene's communications officer.

"What?" snapped the Empress, watching the battle raging about them on the main view screen intently.

"We have a message from Core Central, Exalted One."

"Tell them I'll call back," said Arlene.

"It is important, Exalted One," the communications officer sounded nervous as every head on the bridge swivelled to him. Nobody corrected the Empress and lived.

"We are in the middle of a battle," pointed out Ataar Rizian, "What can be more important than that?"

"Exalted One, the Bugs have invaded the Three Moons of Kandahar and are heading en masse for the Core," said the communications officer very quickly.

The bridge fell silent. Arlene blanched and looked at Ataar, and he whispered, "Atlantis."

"And after that, the Core. If they get to the Core," said Arlene, staring horrified at Ataar, "Damn these Terrans! We should never have left the Core's defences weakened!"

The crew waited, and she looked out at the battle raging around them for a minute, then decided, "Recall the ships. Contact Zokar and tell him we're pulling out. Tell him Atlantis is in danger."

"Yes, Exalted One," said the communications officer, and turned to his console, "All vessels, withdraw, I repeat, retreat. We are needed at home."

"Tell Zokar?" Ataar queried Arlene quietly, puzzled. "What can Zokar do?"

"I'm not sure. But if these humans want an alliance, perhaps Zokar can persuade them to help us against the Bugs," muttered Arlene. Ataar looked dubious. Arlene snapped, "Or is Atlantis's one remaining prince the sort to sit idly by while the Bugs overrun his world?"

"You forget, *Lady*, that Atlantis has both a *king* and a prince," Ataar said to her archly.

On board the Reingold, a message blipped on Elesk's console, and she walked over to Zokar, "Sir, there is a message coming in from the Empress."

"Put it on my viewer," said Zokar curiously. What could the Empress want?

"Zokar?" Arlene's voice was different. There was something other than coldness in it. Was it warmth? Or even fear? Something in her tone drew Zokar's full attention immediately.

"Yes, Arlene?"

"The Bugs....." the link sputtered and faded, and Zokar glared at Elesk until it came back, "... moons of Kandahar. The next ....." it faded again.

Zokar stilled, and snapped to Elesk, "Get it back!"

She fought her console, her face pale, and eventually Arlene's voice came back, "...believe they are heading for Atlantis...."

Zokar and Elesk stared at each other, a chill even greater than the normal chill of elven blood running through both their veins.

Zokar looked around at Shiva, who had been talking intently into his console, but happened to glance at Zokar at that moment. Shiva looked up at him, tilted his head and froze momentarily. Then he jumped out of his chair and strode over to Zokar, then asked, "What is it?"

"The Bugs are swarming. They're headed for Atlantis," said Zokar in a hushed voice, as if still trying to convince himself that it wasn't really happening.

Shiva stared at him blankly, and Zokar whispered, "Shiva, please. We have to go."

Shiva's eyes were tortured, "We can't. Not yet."

"Why not?" asked Zokar.

"I just got word, Laura and Dom have disappeared," said Shiva. "We have to find them."

Zokar's voice was still low, so that only Shiva could hear the unsteadiness in it, "I cannot stay here while my home is destroyed."

Shiva rubbed his tired eyes, "I know."

"What can you do that anyone else can't do to find Dom and Laura?" asked Zokar urgently, "That is assuming they even want to be found?"

"Zokar, there's something you don't know. These Greys, when they suck the life out of everyone-"

"Yes?"

"It doesn't affect me. I seem to be immune. If they have Laura, I am probably the only one who can fight my way through to her and get her back."

Zokar stared at him, then Shiva looked at him, "Go."

Zokar looked at Shiva blankly, "Go?"

"Take one of the blue ships. Go to Atlantis, Zokar. I'll find Laura and sort this mess out, then join you later."

Zokar nodded, slowly, then turned to Elesk, "You heard him. Contact McCosker and get a ship."

"Sir," she said and turned to her console.

"What about Trudi?" asked Shiva, "Do you wish me to have her report to the shuttle bay?"

Zokar looked down, then hesitated and told Shiva, "No. She will hate me for this, but I have no desire to take her into a Bug war, Shiva. Especially not in the initial stages, when they are hungry and swarming."

"I'll look after her."

Zokar turned back to Shiva and met his eyes, "Thank you."

Shiva said, "We have two wars on our hands, now."

Zokar quipped, "You run this one and I'll go take charge of the other one," but his voice sounded a little hollow even to him as he said it, then he turned to leave the bridge of the Reingold with Elesk. Shiva watched him go.

Zokar and Elesk had shuttled across to the Opal ship assigned to them, and were settling in to the bridge. Zokar thought of Trudi and Ghrian. He sighed, glad they were going to be left out here near Earth. He was heading into a Bug war, which he knew would make the war with the Greys look like a Sunday picnic on Earth. He looked around at a bridge full of young strangers, and sighed again. Heading into a war with a bridge crew he did not know, was not Zokar's preference, but he consoled himself with the thought that the fewer friends he took with him, the fewer he would have to watch die. He glanced at Elesk and wondered briefly whether she would survive, whether any of them would, then ordered, "Helm, best speed to the Core."

"Aye, sir."

Best speed in the Opal ships was quite impressive, realised Zokar.

Just then the bridge door dissolved open and admitted two humans that Zokar recognised.

"Hey, Zokar. Need a hand?" grinned the tall footballer Nick.

"Nick, Karl? What are you doing here?"

"General McCosker said you were heading off into a shit fight by yourself. Can't have that, can we?" asked Nick. Karl smiled quietly at Zokar.

Both of them took up positions behind Zokar and stood quietly. It was where Zokar and Gan would have stood behind Shiva, realised Zokar, and it felt odd but comforting to the big elf.

"Thanks," he muttered to Nick. Nick grinned and said, "Don't mention it. Man, these little ships sure can cane that wormhole, can't they?"

Zokar turned to look at him, then looked back at the wormhole, which was twisting about them with an urgent fury that would have buffeted the Reingold to pieces. On the Opal ship, the characteristic vibration of faster than light speed was absent, with only a silky hum at the edge of

Zokar's elvish hearing indicating that they were travelling as fast as they were.

"Yes," said Zokar. Something occurred to him, and he asked Nick and Karl, "Can you even fight?"

"We're from Earth. We can fight," said Nick.

"He's got a jaw breaker of a left hook," observed Karl.

"How do you know that?" asked Zokar.

Karl smiled, "We're friends. He's hit me once or twice."

Zokar looked askance at both the Terrans.

Chapter Twenty-five

Shiva looked up as Trudi entered the bridge of the Reingold.

"What's happening? Why are the Union ships moving off and why did we just send over a shuttle?" she murmured in his ear as she stepped up behind the centre chair.

"There's a situation, at Atlantis."

"A wha-" she glanced at Zokar's empty seat and turned back to Shiva, "Shiva, what the devil is going on? Where's Zokar?"

"Er," said Shiva.

"Shiva!"

"On the shuttle," he replied evasively.

"But the shuttle took off-"

"Trudi, there has been a Bug invasion in the Core and Zokar left to defend his home planet," said Shiva in a rush.

Silence fell, then Trudi whispered, "That bastard! Why didn't he tell me?"

Shiva's eyes flashed with a strange glint and he turned to her, "He's trying to keep you safe. You have no idea what a Bug war can be like!" For some reason his voice sounded strange to Trudi, sending a chill through her spine.

"I'm not a child, Shiva. I can look after myself."

Shiva sighed and nodded, "Some time I will tell you about the Bug wars I have fought in. Not now though. We need to regroup closer in to Earth, to defend ourselves."

"Regroup?" she asked.

"Yes, losing those ships that Zokar took has left us a little short on ships. And the Union ships are leaving. We have only the Earth forces left to defend against the Greys."

Trudi looked thoughtful, and suggested, "Why don't you bring the wagons in a circle?"

"The what?"

"You're defending a lot of empty space, Shiva. Bring the ships in around each planet and moon, around Earth and the Sun. If we make defensive bubbles around each planet we'll save ourselves from defending too much space like we are now."

Trudi always made a lot of sense. Shiva noted for future reference how quickly her Terran mind switched from annoyance at Zokar's departure, to considering their fighting strategy.

Shiva said, "We'll need to be far enough out to get out response barrages in plenty of time…"

"Agreed, but even doing that, it will still save you an enormous number of war ships."

Shiva nodded, and glanced over at Zokar's chair, realizing only after he had done it that he was seeking affirmation of the new strategy from his first officer, a first officer who was not at his post; who was by now many light-years away, racing off to defend his own planet. Shiva tightened his mouth and set his jaw. He had commanded on his own plenty of times before. Why, he wondered, did he have an odd sense of foreboding about it this time?

Chapter Twenty-six

War in space consists largely, thought Zokar, of getting there. Even the blue Opal ships could not reach Atlantis fast enough for him, and he paced the small bridge restlessly, watching the twisting stars, which crawled past too slow for his liking. Eventually they came to the Core systems. Zokar could pick out the familiar constellation of which Atlantis was part.

Nick said, "I like these blue ships."

"Why?" asked Zokar.

"I don't get space sick on them," replied Nick.

Karl grinned, "You should have seen him on the Galactic Union battle cruiser. He was green."

"They do travel well," agreed Zokar. It was a relief to know that, even if this Terran crew was a little inexperienced in space battle, they would not be crawling around the floor vomiting when he needed them to fire off missiles.

The relief crew for the security detachment arrived on the bridge. Zokar flicked a glance at them, and the skin on the back of his neck prickled as his silver hackles rose. He leaned over to Nick and whispered, "Who are they?"

"Oh, new security team. They just enlisted, could hardly wait to get into battle. Australians."

Zokar took a surreptitious look at the tanned faces and hard, quick eyes of the team. They looked a mixture of all Terran races, but there was a consistently dangerous air about them all. They looked hard, and muscled, and ready to fight, with the gleaming eyes of the very fit. Zokar asked Nick quietly, "What are they, mercenaries?"

"Nope, just ordinary citizens."

"Australia; that's that desert continent in the Southern hemisphere, isn't it? But I thought it was quite peaceful."

Nick grinned, "It is now. It was originally a convict settlement, where they shipped all the worst criminals on Earth for a hundred years or so."

Zokar frowned, and leaned back, staring openly at the Australians, "So on your prison planet, where we incarcerated the most intractable criminals in the galaxy, these were the ones you considered needed to be sent off to a prison continent?"

"That about sums it up," smiled Nick.

The Australians as a group flashed white-toothed smiles at Zokar when they noticed his scrutiny, and he turned back to the view screen. His hackles stayed up though, annoying him.

They made contact with a Bug ship convoy only an hour later. Zokar ordered them to come out of hyperdrive a few light-years in front of the convoy.

"How many ships?" asked Zokar, his eyes gleaming in anticipation.

"About fourteen, sir," answered the scanning technician.

"We could take them," said Zokar thoughtfully, then ordered, "Helm, take us straight past them and drop out of hyperdrive in front of them, facing the same direction. I want them to think we've come out of hyperdrive and not seen them."

Nick stared at him, "They'll see us!"

"I want them to see us. I want them to chase us," Zokar said, "They'll bunch up."

The helmsman did as directed, and Zokar pursed his lips with satisfaction as the massive Bug ships powered up in pursuit of the tiny Opal ship. Obviously, the Bugs saw them as easy pickings, a small blue ship alone in space.

"They're going maximum speed," smiled Zokar. Nick was watching him like a hawk, learning. The

Ausstralians were watching his every move, too, the elf noticed. Zokar commanded, "Take us into hyperdrive."

The blue ship accelerated into the wormhole with barely a shudder, and Zokar waited until the Bug ships all followed into hyperdrive, "Ah, Bug navigators," he smiled coldly, "They're so easy to mess with. Helm, speed up slowly, tell me when their speed plateaus."

The blue ship sped up slowly, the Bug ships powering up in hot pursuit. But the blue ship was still accelerating easily when the helmsman said, "They've plateaud, I think they're at full speed."

"Give me ninety five per cent of their full speed," commanded Zokar.

There was a silence as the helmsman complied. Nick looked curious, "Why are we going slower than them?"

"I want them to think they can catch us," smiled Zokar.

Nick frowned and watched, looking fascinated.

"Helm, on my mark, cloak and give me maximum speed, then do a two-seventy, ninety, zero manoeuvre and spread a mine wall across their run," ordered Zokar.

"Sir," agreed the Terran helmsman.

"And... mark!" said Zokar.

The Opal ship disappeared off the scanners of the Bug ships, which continued to pursue its last known course. But invisible to them, the tiny ship shot around sideways then came back across their line of travel, spreading a vertical wall of mines in front of the Bug ships. The Opal ship flew sideways away from the convoy, and was well out of reach when the Bug ships hit the mines.

Explosions bubbled out from nine of the ships immediately. One of the other ships was struck by debris from an adjacent ship and another drifted on an angle in space. The other three ships braked desperately but in doing so became wallowing targets for the darting Opal ship, which flew back in and took out their main engines.

Zokar ordered them back to full speed for the Core,

and Nick stared at him.

Zokar said, "What?"

"Nothing. Just learning," said Nick.

Zokar said, "You are, aren't you? You're always learning, you Terrans."

"You're not going to look for survivors?" asked Nick, and Zokar turned a look on him that made the human feel chilled, and replied, "These are Bugs. No, we do not look for survivors."

"Heading, sir?" asked the helm, and Zokar flicked some buttons on his console and said, "Heading's in, for Atlantis."

When they arrived near Atlantis, the battle line was not hard to find. They came across floating debris from both Union and Bug ships, and Zokar shot some Bugs off the hulls as they went past.

"Are they space-capable?" asked Nick, horrified.

"Bugs? Of course."

"Then why do they need ships?" asked Nick.

"Speed and storage," explained Zokar, "Inside that Bug ship you will find many comatose humans."

Nick glared at the Bug ship, "Why don't we stop and help them?"

"We have tried, in the past. But the atmosphere on those ships is only maintained to keep the humans alive. If we attempt rescue, the Bugs will just open all the airlock doors and fly away, leaving the humans within to die before we can rescue them."

"Christ," said Nick, looking ill.

"And we have enough trouble, without worrying about rescue missions," added Zokar, and then Nick looked at the main viewer and gasped, "My God, the scale of this! There must be tens of thousands of ships out there? What good can we do, with one ship and fifty people?"

Zokar smiled as he looked out at the Bug and Union ships battling each other furiously across the screen, making their tiny blue ship seem like a drop falling into a raging ocean. Zokar knew exactly what he was doing. He had put Elesk on weapons, and both elves were concentrating hard as the tiny ship steered in to the thickest area of fighting, under cloak and ducking in and out of hyperdrive.

"What can I do?" asked Nick.

"Use your human powers. Enhance our defensive shields, blow up any hostiles, and warn me if I don't see something." Zokar's voice was clipped.

Nick said "Okay," and tried his best, but things were moving very fast outside the ship, and he finally understood the advantage that elves have in battle as he watched Zokar's and Elesk's hands flying across the consoles with preternatural speed, as the tiny ship ducked unscathed through the battle zone, shooting down enemy torpedoes and ships and taking out tiny fighters as they went.

They ducked under a huge Bug ship, and Elesk said tightly, "Hit their stabilizers and spin them," to Zokar, who nodded. The blue ship did a quick loop and released a barrage of fire at a particular point on the ship's damaged hull. The great ship listed helplessly. Elesk targeted one side of the ship and sent a quick burst of fire that spun the ship out of control on three axes, rendering it useless in battle and unable to flee.

Zokar's ship turned again and flew in towards the silver and green planet, beautiful from one side, but blackened and dark over half its light side. Nick realized that this must be Atlantis, the dark area being where the explosion of its moon had blasted half of the planet's surface. The Union had done well to stabilize the planet's orbit and keep the atmosphere from being stripped away, and he wondered at the technology which had achieved that feat.

Zokar was speaking into his intercom, and suddenly the harried face of Arlene appeared, "Zokar, am I glad to see you. Your father is down on the planet and we can't reach him. Can you get to the inner city of New Kandahar?"

Zokar asked, "Don't you need help up here?"

"No, you need to find Ataar!"

Zokar nodded and cut the connection, then steered the blue ship down to the surface. Where the huge Union battle cruisers, nor their slower less well armed shuttles, could not reach the surface without getting shot down, the tiny, fast Opal ship could easily slip through the Bug defences. He stood up as they came in to land, and said briefly to Nick, "Help Elesk. I hope you were watching when we came in! That's all the training you"ll be getting."

Zokar saw Nick's face go white, but the human jumped to the main chair, pulled the weapons console around to face him and began firing as they ascended back up through the atmosphere and headed back to join the nearest group of Union ships.

Zokar had snatched a large black bag as he jumped out the airlock door and it swished shut behind him. He landed on soft silver grass and ducked and ran with the bag, heading for cover. Several explosions tracked his path as he ran across the grass, but then there was a large explosion and he realized Nick must have destroyed the ship that was shooting at him with the blue ship's guns. He heard the trill as the blue ship shot away upwards, and found a collapsed wall to duck under and arrange his weapons. He grabbed a communicator and spoke hopefully in elvish into it, and to his relief his father's voice came back to him.

"Zokar?"

"Where are you?"

"The cake shop where your mother used to take you and Elesk," said Ataar, too canny to give out coordinates in a war zone. The cake shop was in the basement of a large high-rise.

"I'm just over in the main park. What's it like between here and there?"

"It's a hot zone. Crawling with Bugs. Watch yourself, son."

"Okay. How many people do you have with you?"

"Just me," said Ataar, and Zokar winced, wondering what size company Ataar had landed with.

"I'll be there in about ten minutes."

"Thanks."

At the remains of the cake shop, amidst dusty grey powder and rubble, Ataar tried to shift, but his leg was pinned under a concrete pillar and he could not move. He could hear the buzzing of Bugs nearby, and sighed, hoping Zokar would get through safely. Zokar would know how badly trapped his father was for two reasons; firstly, because Ataar had not offered to meet him half-way, and secondly, Ataar had said, "Thanks."

Zokar looked around him, rage filling his heart at the destruction of the remaining pristine part of his home planet. The Bugs could not eat Elves, so killed them on sight. Atlantis was merely a strategic point to be destroyed, a source of hostiles to the Bugs and a planet with no intrinsic value to them.

Just then he heard a whirring noise right above him, and spun over to fire at point blank range, but was snatched up by the crushing pincers of a Bug. The Bug flapped strongly and its stinger came towards Zokar. Zokar aimed his disruptor at the Bug's head and blew it off. The body stopped flapping but the pincer still had Zokar and he felt himself begin to fall to the ground, still attached to the Bug. Hastily he disintegrated the rest of the creature except for the pincer, then turned his blaster downwards and fired it continuously at the ground. The power of the disruptor acted like a jetpack and slowed his descent, but it died about five metres above the ground. Zokar hit the ground and rolled over and over, then into a gap under a fallen concrete pylon. The pincer snapped as he landed and fell away. He pulled out his other disruptor and hosed another Bug out of existence, then began crawling furtively along the concrete near the wall, trying to identify any familiar landmarks in the ravaged city blocks which had once been so familiar to him.

He shot eight more Bugs and took cover again. He glanced about and was surprised to see the old steel sign from the cake shop lying in the rubble nearby. Zokar looked around and suddenly realised he had reached the block his father was trapped in. It took him several minutes of searching to find the basement, and he had to push aside a solid fire-door to gain access. The creaking attracted two more Bugs, which he fought off at the entrance. When he pinned the second one to a far wall with a few well-placed arrows, he ducked into the basement and pulled the door closed after him.

"Father!" he called, and was gratified to hear an instant answer, "Zokar?"

Zokar waited for a few seconds to adjust his vision to the dimness, then pushed his way down through the rubble, "Where are you?"

"At the front of the building. I'm trapped under a pillar and some steel reinforcing!" said Ataar.

Zokar grinned as he finally found his father. He looked down at him through the reinforcing grid. "How much ransom will you pay me to get you out, old man?"

Ataar laughed at him, "I see young Shiva's attitudes have rubbed off on you, my noble son!"

"I am at your service, then, you old freeloader," smiled Zokar. He looked around and asked, "How did you get in there?"

"I constructed a cage around myself by attempting to exit the building, which chose that moment to collapse around me," sighed Ataar ruefully. "I have been trying to reach that partial beam beside you to use it as a lever, but to no avail."

Zokar picked up the length of steel beam and said, "Stand back, I'll use this to lever up the mesh."

It was harder than Zokar expected. The mesh was apparently titanium, and he struggled and heaved at it for many long minutes, slowly lifting a small, bent up gap in the mesh. Luckily, he thought, the beam was also titanium and not soft steel. He looked at Ataar, "You should probably be able to get through here now. It's just high enough."

A sudden warning cry came from Ataar and Zokar

spun to see a Bug swoop down towards him. He jammed a rock under the beam he had used as a lever, ducked through the gap in the mesh he had just made, then shot the rock away with his disruptor. The beam and reinforcing mesh dropped back down with a bang and Zokar joined his father.

The Bug hissed and spat with frustration. As it clawed its way off across the rubble again, it dragged the steel post with it, out of Zokar's reach. Zokar said, "I'd better go get that." But just then several more Bugs came swooping down and threw themselves at the two elves behind the mesh, chewing frantically at the titanium. Zokar blasted them. The sky darkened suddenly and they both looked up, only to duck back as thousands of Bugs swarmed down towards their makeshift cage. Zokar blasted as many of them as he could, but after a while said to Ataar, "I'm getting low on charge." As if to confirm his statement, his second blaster sputtered and died just then.

Chapter Twenty-seven

On board the Reingold, the communications panel was lit up. Shiva leaned over it, listening carefully to a barely-audible transmission.

"It's a distress signal from Atlantis," he said, his voice troubled, "They've called for any and all assistance. The Bugs must have been breeding up more than we thought."

Just then another call came through, loud and clear, obviously from closer by.

Shiva looked at his communications officer, who sighed and put the transmission on. "Thees eez the new Terran Alliance Overseer. We have two hostages, Domhan and Laura Keallach, and we demand ransom from you, Captain Shiva, beeefore zey well be released."

Shiva's face went cold, as without hesitation, he said casually, "Slit their throats, see if I care. You'll get no ransom from a Trader." He cut the communication abruptly.

"You bastard!" hissed Trudi, grabbing Shiva by the shoulder and spinning him towards her.

"The Greys will not kill Dom or Laura. They are too rich a food source for them," he said coolly, and wrenched his shoulder away.

"You didn't even ask what ransom they wanted."

"It would have been more than I could afford, I assure you," growled Shiva.

"You can't leave her with them!" she said savagely.

"She is in no immediate danger. They will keep her alive, if only to feed off her. The Galactic Union on the other hand, is in danger: Atlantis is being invaded as we speak."

"Atlantis? That's Zokar's home world, isn't it?" She glared at him, then surmised, "This isn't about saving the Galactic Union. This is about saving Zokar, isn't it?"

"Don't be ridiculous!" spat Shiva. "We have a war on our hands and you think I would consider the safety of one companion over the billions of humans on your planet?

"Oh come on! You know as well as I do that you don't give a rat's arse about the Galactic Union!"

"We cannot leave the Core undefended! Are you mad?"

"Laura will never forgive you for this," she said coldly. "And neither will I."

"Get off my bridge," he told her icily, and she glared at him, glared at the crew around her, then stormed out. Two minutes later the shuttle bay contacted him, "Sir, Trudi St John has manned a shuttle and is requesting clearance to depart for Earth. Shall we apprehend her?"

"No," said Shiva after a moment, "Let her go."

Shiva sighed and turned to the communications console, "General McCosker?"

"Captain Kiran! What can I do for you?"

"I need a fast ship. Zokar Rizian's planet is in trouble."

McCosker said, "Zokar? Hell, son, you can have fifty ships. I'm coming with you."

"Thank you."

Chapter Twenty-eight

Shiva paced the bridge of the Reingold as fifty Opal ships swung away from the Earth fleet and came to surround the listing, damaged ship. He said quietly to Elesk, "Take the Reingold back to Earth for repairs, I will go on one of the Opal ships. This is a mission where speed is essential. Elesk nodded and took the centre seat.

An Opal ship swung into the shuttle bay of the Reingold, and Shiva stepped into the sleek command centre. He stopped himself from glancing to his side where Zokar usually stood, and set his mouth as he saw the damage to the Reingold. From outside the ship it was worse than he had realized.

He said quietly to the navigator, "Set course for Atlantis, best speed."

The navigator nodded and coded in the course, "Standing by, Captain."

"Proceed," said Shiva, and the Opal ship headed for the Core and Atlantis.

The faint hum of top speed hyperdrive surrounded him, as the blue ships escorted them wide of the battling Earth and Grey forces. When they were back in clear space, heading for the Core, he said tiredly, "I'll be in the quarters sleeping. Wake me up if we come across any hostiles."

"Aye, aye, Captain."

Shiva found a free bunk and slept deeply, only waking up to the buzzer of his intercom, "Captain, we are approaching what looks like a major fleet."

"On my way," said Shiva fuzzily, and dragged himself back to the bridge. When he arrived, he ran his hand through his hair and checked the chronometer. He had managed three hours' sleep. It would be enough.

He stared at the view screen, "What the hell? Are those Fey ships?"

The helmsman nodded, "They do fit the configuration, sir. And they are hailing us."

"Put it up."

A group of Fey faces looked at him. Standing in the middle of the group was one in a magnificent silver uniform, resplendent with medals and insignia. Shiva said, "Captain Shiva Koran of the Terran fleet here. State your business and destination."

"Fleet Admiral Tre-kehn. Our destination is Earth. We seek to free our allies from the Grey forces," said the Fey admiral.

Shiva looked at him thoughtfully, "Earth is well defended."

The captain looked blankly at Shiva, "I did not say it wasn't. I said we intend to help free our allies. But tell me, Captain Kiran, why do you flee the battle? You call yourself Terran, yet you are departing at maximum speed from Terra."

"I'm not fleeing this battle, Admiral, I'm heading in to help with another one," sighed Shiva. "The Bugs are swarming and Atlantis is falling as we speak."

There was a sudden flurry of activity and concern among the Fey, and Shiva asked, "How many ships do you have in your fleet?"

Tre-kehn said, "Two thousand, one hundred and forty-two."

"Do you have fuel to get to the Core?"

The Admiral stared at him aghast, "Yes, we refuelled at Orion. But seriously, you do not ask us to help the elvish instead of the humans?"

Shiva stood up and walked up to the view screen, "Your human friends at the Core and on Earth won't stand against the Bugs if Atlantis falls, Admiral, and you know it.

To save them, you first must accompany us and help defeat the Bugs at the Core. To do otherwise would be futile."

Fleet Admiral Tre-kehn stared at him for a long time, and Shiva stared back. Then the Fey man said, "Very well. We will set course and accompany you to Atlantis."

The transmission went blank, and Shiva heaved an unsteady sigh. *At least, he thought, I have a chance of saving Atlantis now with over two thousand ships, rather than just fifty.*

He looked around the bridge and felt the absence of Zokar, Trudi, Laura and even Dom keenly. Even the company of the big cats, Gan and Ghrian, would have been welcome, but scanners had shown that they had departed on the shuttle with Trudi.

Chapter Twenty-nine

Shiva watched intently as their fleet approached the battle raging around Atlantis. Before them were thousands of Galactic Union battle cruisers, packed more densely around the flagship on which he assumed were Arlene and Ataar. Closer in around the planet were Bug vessels, pouring out fire towards the Union ships. A few unidentified alien vessels either fled the fighting or joined in, the only way Shiva could identify them as friendlies or hostiles being the direction of their fire. There was no sign of the blue ship in which Zokar had deployed.

Shiva snapped out an order, "Communications, get me the Empress!"

The face of Arlene appeared almost instantly on his screen, and she railed at him, "Captain Kiran, I see that you have brought more enemies to our gate!"

"The Fey are here to help us, Empress!"

She looked taken aback, and said, "What sorcery do you hold, Captain? How do you turn the minds of men and elves and Fey to your sword?"

"That doesn't matter! Where is Zokar?"

"He is trapped down on the planet below. We had a trace on communications with Ataar who was with him, but that seems to have been blocked."

"Shit!" said Shiva emphatically. "I'm going down after him. Arlene, I'll get communications to patch you through to Fleet Admiral Tre-kehn of the Fey."

"You can't go down there! A human wouldn't last five seconds on the surface!"

"I bring you twenty-two hundred ships, Empress. Don't tell me what I can and can't do."

Shiva left the bridge at a run, saying, "Ready a shuttle!"

Two minutes later he was piloting the shuttle – well, guiding it as it fell would be a more accurate description, because one engine had already been shot off – down to the surface of Atlantis, as close as possible to Ataar's last transmitted position. He could only hope that Zokar had made it to Ataar and both were still alive.

Shiva swore as a swarm of Bugs flew up at him from the ground. He fired on the cluster, but then something hit the shuttle from above and he lost helm control. He threw himself on the floor as the shuttle plummeted to the ground. There was an impact, then pain, then everything went black.

Shiva flexed his fingers as consciousness returned. Rubble fell away from his hands and he pushed himself up, groaned, sank down, then remembered Zokar and pushed himself up to squat on all fours. He was outside the shuttle, which was nowhere to be seen. There was something wrong with his vision, because the colours around him were all wrong. His hands looked blue, and he must be seeing double, because he had four hands.

Shiva groaned again, then saw flashes of light and explosions all around him. He pushed himself to his feet and felt dizzy. The ground seemed too far away. His blaster had disappeared off his hip, and rage began to build within him. It did not stop.

He began walking, not knowing where he was going, but strangely, knowing that this direction would take him to Zokar. A Bug flew at him and he glared at it. Suddenly it disappeared in twin blazes of light, and Shiva swung to look behind him for the ship that had shot it... but there was nothing there. He turned to march doggedly on. His body felt strange and heavy, and his eyes weren't right yet, because his hands still looked blue; all of them. Shiva shook his head to clear it, then almost lost his footing as the ground beneath his feet quaked in response to a large explosion that seemed to come from all around him.

A group of Bugs flew at him, and he glanced at them. They exploded, and so did the building behind them. Shiva shook his head to clear it, and looked around him again, seeking the ship that must surely be protecting him. There was nothing there.

The rough landing must have dazed him more than he thought, he decided.

Chapter Thirty

Zokar looked up. They were trapped, out of ammunition, and the bugs darkened the sky all around them. He turned to his father, and asked, "Any ideas?"

Ataar shook his head numbly. They peered cautiously out from the pile of rubble. The reinforcing of the building they were in had survived, a titanium mesh that had unfortunately buckled from the heat of the repeated blasts and fallen down over them, trapping them like animals in a cage, with a perfect view of death approaching them in the form of the circling Bugs. Their only escape route, a slight lift in the mesh, was blocked by ten crawling Bugs.

"Any friendlies out there?" Ataar asked Zokar hopefully.

"I don't think-," Zokar yelped and jumped backwards as two huge Bugs landed on the titanium mesh he was clinging to, and began to chew determinedly at the mesh. More Bugs landed on the mesh. Zokar and Ataar scrambled back, up the pile of debris behind them, and fell silent, watching death eat its way slowly towards them. A piece of mesh gave way, then another. Zokar glanced past the Bugs, looking for anything; ships, troops... but all he saw was a series of explosions in the distance, coming closer and closer. He drew his sword despite knowing that it would only slow their inevitable demise.

"What's that coming?" he asked Ataar, and Ataar tore his eyes from the Bugs on the mesh to look past them to where Zokar was pointing.

In the distance, buildings fell. Explosions flowered, and the air was orange, blue and white with flames. A tall figure was striding determinedly up the road towards them. Occasionally a group of Bugs would fly towards him, but the figure would let forth twin beams of white fire and strike the Bugs down, so that their blackened and fried carcases plummeted vertically to the ground. The thunderous racket of the fire reached them a second later, the sharp crack and boom making their Elvish ears hurt.

"My God, what is that?" asked Zokar, hands over his ears.

Ataar stared out through the mesh, then answered in a terrified voice, "We have awoken Him."

"Him? Who?" asked Zokar, not comprehending. And hearing the sound of fear in his father's voice was more unnerving to Zokar than he liked to admit. Ataar wasn't even afraid of dragons, so what could possibly make him afraid? "Dammit, Father, you mean there are worse things than dragons on this planet and you didn't see fit to mention it until now?"

"He wasn't on this planet until this morning. He's probably looking for you," explained Ataar.

"What?" asked Zokar, starting to look even more nervous, "Me? What the hell are you on about?" He didn't like the sound of what Ataar was saying. Zokar was forced to consider the very real possibility that his father was suffering shell-shock and losing his wits.

Just then they ducked as the Bugs atop the mesh above them were blasted into oblivion, but suddenly a concerned and familiar voice called out, "Zokar? Are you in there?"

Zokar looked up in shock. Relief ran through his veins like warm water, "It's Shiva!" He called out loudly, "Yes! Shiva! Over here!"

There was a crash and a thump, then the familiar form of his friend landed atop the mesh, and Shiva peered down at them, looking relieved, "Thank God I found you."

Zokar stared up at him, "Man, are we glad to see you!"

Shiva laughed, and said, "Ataar, are you okay?"

"I'm fine, thank you," smiled Ataar. Zokar turned, confused. His father seemed to be back to his usual confident self.

"How did you get through that?" asked Zokar, pulling himself up to the mesh and pointing down the road behind Shiva. "And what are you grinning about?"

"Through what?" asked Shiva, "Zokar, are you alright?"

He pulled and ripped the reinforcing aside like it was paper. Zokar gaped at him. Six bugs had been chewing on that mesh only seconds ago, with thankfully very slow results. How did Shiva, a mere human, rip it like it was paper?

Shiva held out his hand to Zokar and lifted him up out of their prison, and asked, "What happened down the road? Did you guys do that?" He lifted Ataar out and they all stumbled and slid down the rubble to the road.

In a long straight line for several miles from the basement, the rubble was levelled to powder in a swathe cut through the battlefield debris.

"No," said Zokar.

Ataar looked as though something had just dawned on him, "You don't know how that happened? How did you get here, Shiva?"

Shiva scratched his head, and said hesitantly, "I'd been searching for you, but my shuttle was hit. Someone told me you were caught behind the Bug lines and…." he looked a little flustered, "I remember getting here…"

Ataar shrugged, and patted Shiva and Zokar on the shoulders, "It's alright. It's a war zone. Things are bound to get confusing."

Shiva smiled and said, "Come on, let's get back to the shuttles. The war seems to be going our way, by the way, for those of you who have been sitting it out on the sidelines."

Zokar swatted him over the head.

"Ow!" protested Shiva.

"I wouldn't do that," Ataar warned Zokar, looking at Shiva warily.

"Look!" cried Zokar, staring up at the sky. Thousands of small silvery white ships were ducking and weaving around the sky, shooting Bugs as they went.

"The Fey?" asked Ataar, his mouth falling open, "What are they doing here?"

"I asked for their help," shrugged Shiva.

"Fey and elves do not help each other," Ataar shook his head in wonder, staring up at the sky.

Shiva said quietly, "Until we start thinking of each other as Galaxians, not Fey or Elves or humans, we will get nowhere fast in this war, Ataar."

"What's a Galaxian?" asked Zokar.

"We all are," said Shiva, then pointed up at the Fey ships, "So are they."

"You made that up," accused Zokar.

"Actually, you're right," said Shiva, "I did just make that up."

Ataar shook his head at the pair of them, and they made their way down the ruined road back through the decimated city, towards the shuttles which were beginning to drop out of the sky and search for survivors.

Shiva tapped Zokar on the arm, "Good to see you."

"Hmph," said Zokar.

"Has he always been like that?" Shiva asked Zokar's father.

Ataar looked at him blankly, "You mean so sentimental? Yes, he has actually."

Shiva laughed at them both and they shot each other puzzled glances as they followed the human. Zokar rubbed his head, wondering whether he had taken a knock to the head in the battle without realizing, or whether Shiva had.

Chapter Thirty-one

They left Atlantis to the Galactic Union and the Fey, and took one of the Opal ships back to the Solar system. Ataar offered to come with them, to Shiva's surprise and Arlene's displeasure. The mopping up operation was simplified by the fact that they didn't have to take prisoners from the Bugs and process them; they simply blasted the rest of the Bug ships out of existence. Now that Atlantis was relatively safe, Shiva was worried about what had happened back at Earth. He hoped the Reingold was still intact, and that Laura and Dom had been found.

Shiva sat staring at the view screen before him, as though he could will the sleek blue ship along faster than the wormhole of hyperdrive could drag it. Zokar said suddenly, "There!" and they saw a small group of ships.

"They're Grey ships," said Shiva, feeling sick to his stomach.

"And Terran!" exclaimed Zokar, and they stared at the screen, puzzled, as the mixture of blue Opal ships and Grey vessels grew steadily larger on the screen.

"So someone's won the battle, but who?" pondered Shiva.

Zokar was silent beside him, and whispered, "I'm sorry, Shiva. If you hadn't come to help Atlantis-"

"If I hadn't come to help Atlantis, every elf between here and the outer Centaurus arm would have been slaughtered by the Bugs by now, and the Bugs would be heading for the Core. We knew the Greys wouldn't destroy Earth; it's their harvesting ground," said Shiva, meeting Zokar's eyes. Shiva did have a mildly puzzled look on his face, though. That was the first time he had ever heard Zokar apologize for anything.

Then Shiva turned to his communications officer and said, "Hail those ships, identify us and ask them for safe passage. But get ready to fight our way out, just in case."

"Or run," added Zokar, pointing at the monitor on the left of the main view screen. A flock of several hundred ships now showed on the viewer, blue and grey, moving up to surround them.

Shiva slapped his console and announced, "Captain Shiva Kiran to Grey ships, requesting safe passage to Earth. We do not intend hostilities."

"What, are we just going to hand ourselves over to them on a platter?" asked Zokar in his ear.

"Under the circumstances, yes. It is the only way to find out what happened," said Shiva.

Zokar sighed and pursed his lips, then glanced at Ataar, who was frowning at Shiva.

The viewer flicked on, showing a Grey alien of indeterminate age. He looked silently at Shiva and said, without greeting or explanation, "You haff noooo aaaura."

"What?" asked Shiva, taken aback by the odd comment.

"I said, Captain Shiiiva Kiraaan, you haff noooo aaaura."

"That's nice. Can we go to Earth?" Shiva shot Zokar a quizzical look which quite clearly said, "What was that about?" Zokar shrugged. Greys were strange creatures.

"You are welcooome, to our plaaanet."

Shiva sat back and folded his arms, "*Your* planet?"

"*Our* plaaanet," and the Grey alien smiled at him before flicking off the viewer.

Zokar and Shiva exchanged looks, and Zokar said, "Well, that answers the question as to who won the battle. Now, do you have a plan?"

Shiva was silent.

Zokar shook his head, "I didn't think so."

They headed in past the distant giant Jupiter and came across another group of about twenty ships making its way out of the Solar system towards the Core. The small flotilla slowed to contact them.

Domhan Keallach's face appeared on their viewscreen, surrounded on his bridge by elves and Fey, but no humans or Greys, noted Shiva.

"Dom! Where are Laura and Trudi?"

"Greetings Ataar, Captain Kiran, Zokar. I am afraid that information is classified," replied Domhan in an infuriatingly haughty manner.

Shiva's eyes narrowed dangerously and Dom squirmed a little under the captain's gaze.

Zokar stepped forward beside Shiva, who did not look capable of speech. Murder, perhaps, but not speech.

Zokar asked Dom, "What happened here, my Lord?"

"I took the necessary actions to prevent a war," replied Dom, evenly.

Zokar frowned, "What actions?"

"What the Hell did you do, Dom?" Shiva was standing up now, his hot temper finally beginning to flare, glaring at Dom.

Dom hung his head, and said, "I did that which was within my purview as proprietor of the Solar system, a sovereign entity of the Galactic Union."

Ataar's eyebrows lifted, but he remained silent and watched the situation play out before him.

"Bullshit. Earth's not a part of the Galactic Union and you know it! *What did you do?*" demanded Shiva.

"The Greys of Andromeda have taken the first step in become citizens of the Galactic Union. They have... purchased property here," answered Dom, as if that explained everything.

"Property? What property? Ships?" A thought occurred to Shiva, and he growled dangerously, "Tell me you didn't sell them the Reingold."

"No. I said property," said Dom.

"What?" asked Shiva and Zokar as one, but Shiva was beginning to feel sick to his stomach. He said to Dom, "What did you sell them?"

"Earth."

Chapter Thirty-two

"What the Hell? You can't do that!" said Shiva, astounded.

Zokar had fallen silent.

Shiva stared at the impassive face of Domhan Keallach.

Ataar finally spoke up softly, "Actually, he can."

Shiva turned to Ataar, incomprehension in his eyes, "What?"

"He is a Keallach by blood descent. Technically, his family owns the entire galaxy. And the Galactic Union has never recognised the sovereignty of the New Terran Empire. Legally, Earth is still Galactic Union property; his property, to sell if he wishes," Ataar spoke quietly, but there was something dark in the silver eyes as he looked back at Dom.

Shiva turned to stare at Dom, "What sort of a-? You can't just sell Earth off like a ranch with so many prize cattle!"

"As the Galactic Regent, Lord Ataar Rizian, has just pointed out, Captain Kiran, indeed I can. Especially if it was necessary to prevent the wholesale slaughter and destruction of a system-wide war."

"But they won't stop! Dom, they won't stop at Earth! The Greys will be looking for the rest of the human planets next! You haven't stopped a war, you've just given the enemy a foothold! You've given them a base in our galaxy! Are you mad?"

Dom shrugged, and said, "Part of the deal was an undertaking by the Greys not to target the rest of the Galactic Union."

Shiva glared at him in disgust, then changed tack, "For God's sake, Dom, at least tell me where Laura is?"

"And Trudi," added Zokar, in a soft voice which made the bridge crews of both ships shudder. Even Ataar raised a surprised eyebrow at his son at the ice in his tone.

"I don't think so," said Dom, coldly.

Shiva stared at him, "So you bought your own freedom, and the Union's, but not Earth's? Not your sister's?"

Dom looked away and said, "You do not understand me at all, Captain. If you think-" then he seemed to stop himself, but the dark blue eyes bored into Shiva's with an intensity that produced a puzzled frown from the human captain. But after a moment, Dom looked puzzled too, and turned in desperation to stare instead at Zokar. Shiva frowned and glanced at Zokar.

Zokar just continued to glare at Dom, who stared at them both oddly, then said, "You two are different."

"Don't change the subject," seethed Shiva.

"I am not. You, Shiva, you are like a blank wall. And Zokar, you have no soul to see." Dom was looking at them both like he was seeing them for the first time. Then he shook himself and said dismissively, "I must return to the Core to ratify this treaty with the Greys, gentlemen. I trust that we shall meet again shortly."

Their viewer went blank, and Shiva said to Zokar, "What the hell was that about?"

"I have no idea," said Zokar, "But I will say this: his behaviour is inconsistent."

"How so?" asked Shiva, turning his chair to look at Zokar.

"Why would he spend eighteen years searching for his sister, then desert her now?"

Shiva frowned, and said, "I don't know. What's he playing at?"

"He of all people would know how helpless Laura is, as a prisoner of the Greys. Perhaps it is some sort of ruse, a play for time? Or perhaps he felt it was the only peaceable option open to Earth?"

"Or perhaps he just decided to save his sorry hide and split!"

Zokar frowned, and shook his head slowly, "Perhaps once I would have ventured a guess as to his motives, but now, I do not know enough about Dom to hazard such a guess. In fact," and he frowned and looked up, "Nobody really knows that much about Domhan Keallach now at all, do they?" He looked enquiringly at Ataar, who merely shook his head.

"He's Laura's twin, and we know a lot about Laura," suggested Shiva.

"Do we? Do we really?" asked Zokar.

They powered on past the tiny red planet Mars, towards Earth, unsure what they would find.

"That's strange," said Zokar, staring into his scanners.

"What?" snapped Shiva.

"We should be in scanning range of Earth now, but…."

"Magnify main viewer to maximum using long range scanners," said Shiva to the communications officer impatiently.

The scant stars on the viewer seemed to leap forward at them, but instead of the beautiful blue jewel of Earth which had so entranced both Shiva and Zokar upon first seeing it on their initial arrival at Earth in the Reingold many months before, all they could see was a vast grey cloud.

"What the devil is that?" asked Shiva, standing up and peering at the view screen.

Zokar was the first to realise, "Ships."

"Oh my God," whispered Shiva, suddenly realising what they were looking at, "There must be millions of them."

"Billions," corrected Zokar.

The grey cloud before them was indeed Earth, but it was now obscured by a cloud of Grey ships, gathered around the beautiful blue planet like bees around a hive, so thick that the planet could not be seen from space.

Shiva sat back in his chair, and sighed, "No wonder Dom capitulated. How in the name of creation do you fight that?"

Zokar looked at him, wondering suddenly if even his captain was going to give up this battle before it started. Shiva, who was wondering exactly the same thing, met Zokar's eyes with a lost expression that spoke volumes, and they both stared back at the ominous cloud around Earth. Parasites, Shiva reminded himself. They are parasites. It was Shiva's turn to shudder, then he sat forward and rubbed his hand tiredly over his face. He ended up sitting with his hand over his mouth, sighing into his hand and making a hissing sound.

Zokar knew that gesture; Shiva was considering all the options before him, conjuring up and dismissing strategies, shuffling through the arsenal of tactical approaches that nested deep within the captain's mind, thinking hard. Eventually Shiva sat forward with a hard gleam in his blue eyes, and said, "Parasites."

Zokar stepped down to the command chair, and asked, "Parasites?"

"They live off the humans' telepathic output, right?"

"Right."

"Well, we can't fight them physically, but what if we could figure out a way to starve them out?"

"How? Even a sleeping human puts out telepathic emissions."

"There's one human we know who doesn't," mused Shiva. He turned to meet Zokar's eyes.

"Who?"

"Me. And we have yet to find out why," replied Shiva.

"Even Laura couldn't figure that out," agreed Zokar, "Maybe if we could figure out why the Greys can't draw on your mind, we could figure out a way to stop them drawing on other human minds? But we need a guinea pig. How are we going to do this?"

"Laura's not human. To figure out how to deal with the Greys, we need someone totally human, with a really analytical mind," said Shiva.

The looked at each other, and said at the same time, "Trudi!"

"Yeah, but where the hell is she?" asked Shiva.

""I wish I knew," sighed Zokar. He missed Trudi, more than he would ever admit.

"I bet she's with Laura," said Shiva. "But how do we find them?"

"They won't show on scanners. There are too many mixed life forms down there, human, elvish, Fey, now. And the power emissions from Laura would be being sucked up by these Greys.

Shiva suddenly thumped the arm of his chair, "The cats! Gan and Ghrian!"

"What about them?" asked Zokar, puzzled.

"They went on the shuttle with Trudi!" exclaimed Shiva. "And Laura told me they are not Earth cats, remember?"

"That's right. We should be able to scan for the cats. I'll get onto it straight away. I'll bet Trudi has found Laura, and I'll bet she took the cats with her to find her," said Zokar.

Shiva nodded. At least if they could find Laura and Trudi, perhaps they could figure out some way of preventing the Greys from draining the psychic energy from the humans. If not, with a bit of luck they could escape the system and get help from the Core. He wondered briefly if that was what Domhan Keallach was planning to do; go to the Core and bring back the fleet.

It took hours of patient scanning, but eventually Zokar located the two cats, deep underground.

"Where?" asked Shiva.

"A place called Egypt. The Valley of the Kings. There are massive tombs there, and the cats are showing up as being deep underground in one of them," said Zokar.

"Well, whatever," shrugged Shiva, "I'll need a task force, say forty. Get one of the new Five series shuttles ready. It needs to be a new shuttle."

"Very well," said Zokar, and stood up from his chair to follow Shiva. Shiva said, "No, no, you'd better stay here, Zokar. I can't risk both of us."

The look that Zokar gave his captain made Shiva lean back a little.

Zokar said, "Begging your pardon, Captain."

"Yes, First Officer?"

"Sir, might I remind you that the Greys can incapacitate all other humans except you, without even touching them. You will require solely elvish and Fey members on your task force," the silver eyes were glittering.

The others stared at Zokar, then Shiva. They were enthralled at Zokar's insubordination. Yet Shiva could understand Zokar's reasons: last time Zokar had let his captain go planetside alone on Earth, Shiva had nearly been killed numerous times, and had been marooned for three months, missing presumed dead.

"Oh, very well, Zokar. But stay out of trouble this time, hey?"

Zokar's mouth dropped open, and the navigator and helmswoman both chuckled, then clammed up quickly as he glared at them, before leaving the bridge two paces behind Shiva. Ataar fell into step behind them, and his team of silent elves followed. The human members of the crew breathed a collective sigh of relief as the tall silver-eyed high elves left the bridge.

"Talkative lot, aren't they?" grinned the helmsman, but then shut up quickly as their superior glared at him.

They arrived at Earth and waited hours for permission to send down a shuttle. Once in the atmosphere, Shiva lost them in the traffic and swung off course.

The shuttle landed on the desert sands, a few miles from the great pyramids. Shiva hit a button and the doors opened. The elves hit the sand at an easy jog, Shiva and

Zokar leading them. The shuttle pilot hit a button on the console and the shuttle burrowed underground like a giant dung beetle in seconds. Shiva and Zokar jogged easily and quickly across the sands in the moonless night, the elves loping silently behind them.

Shiva stopped behind a huge stone structure, and Zokar pointed out the entrance to the pyramid. He looked at Shiva and asked, "Quiet or noisy?"

Shiva did not answer, and Zokar realised that the human was staring entranced at the night sky. "There she is," whispered Shiva.

Zokar looked up and eventually saw what Shiva had; the characteristic pattern of lights that outlined the massive Reingold. From down here on Earth the great ship was a miniscule pattern of hull lights, visible only on a moonless night like tonight. They had not been able to see her through the cloud of Grey ships in orbit.

Shiva looked back down, into Zokar's eyes, and his eyes widened.

"What?" asked Zokar.

"Your eyes are black. I never get used to that."

"Elvish night vision, like any other, is not achieved without expansion of the pupil, Shiva. And you, my friend, can see in the dark better than any human should be able to."

Shiva raised his eyebrows and shrugged innocently.

Zokar drew Shiva's mind back to their mission, "Are we going in hot or cold?"

"Better go in cold. These Greys aren't good fighters, but we don't want them whisking the girls away before we get to them. You, Zetani and Xander, take five elves and cover the back entrance. Everyone memorised the schematics?"

There were general nods.

"When you hear a ruckus, either they've caught us or we're coming out hot. Once we have Laura and Trudi, we'll go for speed rather than stealth."

"I can't see Gan and Ghrian coming out quietly,"

observed Zokar, and Shiva nodded.

"Once we're out, this is our rendezvous point, right here. I'll call the shuttle up once we have the prisoners. All clear?"

Everyone nodded, and Shiva slunk towards the pyramid's base with Zokar, Ataar and the remaining elves like silver ghosts at his heels.

Once they were at the pyramid entrance, Shiva waved the elves back, then strolled up to the guard, "Hi, got a moment?"

The Grey guard stared up at him and asked, "What are you doeeng here? Thees area is out ov bounds."

"Now, that's where we have to agree to disagree," said Shiva mildly, and sheared the guard's head off with a single knife stroke.

The other guards had heard them, but by then they were surrounded by the silent elves, who dispatched them quickly. Shiva smiled his approval as Ataar took a single swing with his sword and neatly beheaded three Greys.

The doors began to slide shut before them, but Zokar jammed his sword between them and they all ducked through the gap and jogged into the corridors, into inky blackness. Zokar drew his second sword as he ran.

If they had been expecting to find the corridors empty, they were sadly mistaken. Almost immediately, they ran into resistance. The short Grey aliens had excellent night vision, and came at them out of the darkness yowling with anger. Shiva lost count of the number of pale limbs he sliced off with his knife, which was covered with the black blood of the little aliens from tip to hilt. His hands were slippery with blood, and he pulled a rag from his belt and hastily wiped off the handle and blade as they stopped at a doorway. He grinned at Zokar as they hear chains clinking and a loud roar just up ahead, "Gan!" Zokar smiled and borrowed the rag, wiped his sword hilt dry and threw down the sodden rag.

"Come on!" smiled Shiva, and they sprinted down the narrow corridor into a small vault. It was packed with Greys, and rather than try to fight them all, Shiva aimed his blaster at the locks on the two cages at the back of the room and the cats sprang out, slashing and biting left and right at Greys, days of pent-up feline rage driving their ferocity. While the big cats kept the Greys busy, Zokar blasted loose the bindings of the two figures laid out on slabs in the middle of the room, and pulled the solid gold helmets off their heads. Shiva and Zokar slung Laura and Trudi over their shoulders and with the cats leading the way, jogged back along the corridors. Zokar grinned as he heard Shiva chopping left and right at the pale suckered hands of screaming Greys, and found himself trotting along over a trail of Grey three-fingered hands behind Shiva.

They emerged into the now surprisingly bright evening, and found the shuttle swinging around and blasting away at the ground defences of the Greys. Gan and Ghrian leapt into the shuttle, then turned around and pulled Zokar and Shiva up easily with their claws, hooking them by the shoulder harnesses and pulling them up with their burdens. The other elves leapt lightly up into the shuttle, the doors slammed, and the shuttle took off with breathtaking speed.

The pilot was saying "Rendezvous point, inside Mars orbit..."

"What the hell?" asked one of the elves, then blanched as the wormhole exploded around them, lifting sand into the air by several thousand feet. They howled on through the wormhole, leaving the Greys confused, stumbling around through sand and darkness with nothing to fight.

Shiva grinned, "The Terrans thought a few warp-capable shuttles would be useful for jobs like this one."

"Hmm," said a couple of the elves, nodding. Zokar smiled. In elvish, that was high praise.

A weak voice beneath him asked Shiva, "Shiva? Zokar? Is Trudi alright?"

"Fine," came a whisper from beside her, "But I think I might need to sleep for a bit...."

Shiva and Zokar lowered the girls into the pull down bunks at the back of the shuttle, and Zokar checked them, and commented, "I don't like what these Greys do to humans. They should be okay, though. They'll just need a few days' rest."

Shiva nodded, and Ataar looked thoughtfully at the human, "Tell me, Shiva, where did you learn to fight?"

Shiva blinked, "I can't remember."

Ataar nodded and smiled, and Zokar shot him a frown at the odd question and response.

"Now where?" asked Zokar, as they approached their beautiful blue ship.

"The Core," said Ataar, then looked slightly abashed as Shiva and Zokar looked at him, "That is if Captain Kiran agrees."

"Why?" asked Shiva.

"We can't do anything here, the Greys are too numerous. The humans can't fight them, we need elves and Fey to fight them. And until the battle at the Core is completely won and every last Bug cleared out of the inner systems, no elf or Fey will leave Atlantis."

Shiva pursed his lips and nodded slowly, but asked, "But what about Earth?

Ataar says, "Let the Greys keep Earth for now, they will keep the Bugs away from it until we have defeated them and driven them out of the Galaxy. We'll come and take Earth back after the war."

"Let's get going before the girls wake up and have a chance to disagree," suggested Shiva, and Zokar nodded his approval. They filed out of the shuttle onto the blue ship, and it was only then that Zokar realized he was bleeding from several wounds. He wiped silver blood off his arm to see how bad the injury was.

"Hah," said Shiva, noticing.

"What?" asked Zokar.

"I got five new scars. You only got three."

The elf scowled at him as the medics began to work

155

on them as they strode back towards the bridge.

"Child," accused Ataar, and Zokar grinned and made a rude elvish hand gesture at him. There was a scuffle from behind Shiva, and Shiva snapped, "Stop it!"

The two elves ducked their heads and followed him, glaring at each other.

Shiva grumbled, "Galaxies! You two, one minute you're running battle fleets and ruling empires, the next minute you're squabbling like two year olds. What is wrong with you elves?"

For some reason, all the elves burst out laughing, and Shiva turned his glare on all of them, then complained "Ouch," as his movement caused the medic trying to keep up with him, to accidentally miss a stitch and pull awkwardly on a wound on his elbow.

They turned the fast Opal ship back towards the Core. On the way, they passed many ship hulks and small pockets of fighting that made it obvious that the Greys had now encountered the vanguard of the Bug invasion and the two factions were involved in fierce fighting, "That will work in our favour," commented Ataar, and Shiva and Zokar agreed.

"They'll keep each other occupied," commented Zokar.

"They're competing for the same food source," said Shiva grimly, and Ataar and Zokar cocked their heads at him. Shiva explained, "Humans."

Chapter Thirty-three

But when they got back to Atlantis, things were not fully under control as they expected. The Bugs continued to pour in from the far side of the galaxy, and Arlene's face on the viewer was harried as she updated them. "We can't deal with the numbers, Ataar. We need the help of the Ancient Ones."

Ataar went pale, but agreed with Arlene, "I'll go down and call them."

Shiva turned around and looked at Zokar, whispering, "Ancient Ones?"

Zokar explained as they travelled back down to the surface of Atlantis in a warp-capable shuttle. "The Ancient Ones are the oldest occupants of Atlantis, but once awoken, they are unpredictable. They consider the elves beneath them, with the exception of a few."

"What few?"

"My father is one of the ones they will deal with."

"And you?"

"I would rather not deal with them at all, but if anything can save Atlantis, they can." But Zokar's knew his eyes must look haunted as the shuttle approached the ground of Atlantis, for Shiva kept looking at him quizzically.

Shiva jumped out of the shuttle and ran for cover with Zokar and Ataar, "Are you sure this is where they are?"

"Yes," said Ataar, "I grew up in this area."

Zokar felt his hackles rise, and he knew his face was set and grim. He looked around them constantly. Ataar began walking, leading them up into the hills. Occasionally Ataar would stop and sniff the air, then continue more slowly or change course. Shiva kept close to Zokar.

Zokar knew that Shiva's nose was not as good as the elves' but soon even the human commented, "I smell fire." Zokar had been smelling the whiff of carbon on the breeze for many minutes by then. Ataar held up a hand and stopped them all. They were in the middle of a hilltop. The hilltop was grassed, and unlike the other countryside they were walking through, here the grass was long, coming up to their waists. Around them loomed several large, round granite outcrops, worn smooth over the millennia.

"Don't move," warned Ataar, and Shiva stood staring around them.

"There's nothing here," he whispered to Zokar.

Zokar ran his hand across the waist high grass and answered, "Exactly. Nothing grazes here and there are no flying creatures to be heard."

"Shh!" hissed Ataar, and stood tall.

Shiva stared at him, then Zokar saw something that made his blood run cold. Ataar was standing perfectly still, but every few seconds his hair would be blown back from his face, like something invisible was breathing on it from inches away. Then a voice as deep and ancient as the hills sounded from before them. "Ataar?" The voice seemed to come out of the air.

"Pyrrhus, it has been a long time," said Ataar, in a quiet voice.

"Not to me it has not. A few hundred years," said the deep voice, dismissing the time as though it were several weeks, not several centuries.

Just then Zokar felt warm breath across his own face and saw the air before him shimmer slightly into the forms of two enormous slitted eyes. His body froze in instinctive reaction, and he felt his own hair blown back from his face. He looked across to Shiva and saw the human shudder as their eyes met. Zokar felt the voice vibrate through his bones, sending chills up and down his spine.

"You bring your son," rumbled another voice, from

inches before Zokar. It was female, but still deep and resonating. The voice continued, "So like you. But who is this outworlder? He is a strange one indeed."

"I'm Shiva Kiran," said Shiva, clearly, but respectfully, taking his cue from Ataar.

"Do not take form, Vulcana, for he could destroy us," warned the first voice.

"What?" asked Shiva.

"What do you want, you and your dangerous friend?" asked Pyrhhus.

Ataar answered, "Have you seen what is happening in the world, my lord?"

Zokar saw Shiva's eyes widen as he jumped in response to feeling something, and at the same time Zokar felt hot, silky hide brush past his shoulders from behind. It brushed past him, and brushed past him some more. It felt like forever before the sensation stopped.

"Can we keep this one? Is he a gift?" asked the female voice from right next to Shiva.

"No!" snapped Zokar, suddenly finding his voice.

Vulcana's voice was amused, "Ah, so your son has courage when he needs it. To be expected, of course, being your son."

"When he needs it," chuckled Pyrrhus.

"My lord Pyrhhus, we need your help," said Ataar, making warning eyes at Shiva and Zokar, who subsided into silence.

"We have been helping, frying those giant wasps. Unfortunately, they do not make good eating," sighed Pyrrhus, "Only good sport."

"Then you must help. If they succeed, there will be nothing left here except those tasteless creatures. They are eating all the humans and Elves and livestock, and will not stop until there is no more food for you, Pyrrhus my lord," said Ataar.

There was a long rumble, and Ataar turned to look into Zokar's eyes, holding his breath.

Then Pyrrhus spoke, "What can we do? We are only dragons."

"You are dragons who can awaken my friend," sighed Ataar, and turned to Shiva, whose eyes began to glow a deeper blue than usual. "Seek his mind. You will find it hard to find, but when you do-"

"Father?" said Zokar, worried. This conversation was going in a direction which he had not expected. What had Shiva to do with the Ancient Ones?

Shiva's hair blew back from his face suddenly and Zokar moved towards him, but then found he could not move again. Zokar growled, "Ataar, what the hell are you talking about?"

"Look at me," said the hypnotic voice of the dragon, and suddenly Shiva began to shimmer.

Zokar cried out, "Leave him alone!"

The grass around Shiva was shimmering and changing too. His shimmering body became a pinpoint of bright light, as Zokar fought his frozen limbs and drew his disruptor.

Ataar cried, "Zokar, no!" and Zokar stopped, confused. Ataar assured him, "They can't hurt him!"

"What's happening to me?" asked Shiva, holding his hands away from him nervously.

"You are coming through the planes of existence to us," whispered the dragon's deep voice.

"Zokar?" Shiva asked, shakily, as he seemed to shimmer out of existence.

"Give him back!" roared Zokar, as Shiva faded into nothingness.

"No, Zokar!" cried Ataar, launching himself at Zokar to restrain him as he aimed his disruptor at the last place he had seen the dragon. Zokar struggled, then stilled as Shiva's voice came from in front of his face and he felt hot human hands holding his arms steady.

Shiva's voice told Zokar, "Be still. I'm fine."

Zokar said, "Shiva? Are you alright?"

"I'm fine, Zokar. You have some interesting friends."

Zokar said, "You sound different. And your hands; they feel hotter than human hands, and too big."

"Zokar, stay with Ataar and do what he tells you. I will be back in a day or so."

Zokar lifted his hands to meet the human's invisible ones and nodded, then released Shiva and stepped back. Then he felt coldness and silence, and a sudden absence in the air about them, and looked to his father for confirmation.

Ataar relaxed visibly and nodded at Zokar, "They're gone."

"Will Shiva be alright? They won't hurt him?" asked Zokar.

Ataar smiled cryptically, "I'd be more worried that he"ll hurt them."

"What?" asked Zokar, but Ataar didn't answer and started setting up camp.

Zokar sat on a rock, feeling out of his depth.

But then he felt a puff of hot breath on his hand, and he said in a strangled tone of voice, "Father, they're back."

Ataar frowned, and then smiled, "Lavelle, Ignato, how are you my little friends?"

Then Ataar fell to the ground, knocked down but laughing, and suddenly Zokar was face to scales with a dragon, its scales crystalline and sparkling, its huge green eyes catlike and slitted.

"Hello, I'm Ignato, who are you?" asked the dragon.

"I'm Zokar," said Zokar, trying to get his wits back. He glanced at Ataar, who was pulling himself off the ground by the holding the scales of a second dragon. The dragon bounded happily away as soon as Ataar stood up, then Zokar's attention was drawn back to a barrage of questions and hot breath in front of him.

"Are you Ataar's son? Pyrrhus is my dad. Is your dad as strict as mine? Who's your friend that went with mum and dad? He's really scary."

Zokar tried to make sense of the rapid fire questions, "Yes, Ataar is my father. He used to be pretty strict, and Shiva? Why is he scary? He's just a human."

The dragon snapped its eyes around to meet his, "Just a human? A human who steps between the planes like a dragon, who holds the strands of reality with his hands and toys with them like my father plays with fire?"

Zokar stared at the young dragon, and said, "Shiva? Shiva doesn't do that. What are you talking about? Shiva is the least psychic of us all." He sighed and settled down on a rock, feeling more and more lost, then looked at his father, "You are sure he will come back, aren't you, father?"

"Of course he's safe," said Ataar, "Stop worrying, it's undignified."

"Why can I see them, when I couldn't see their parents?" asked Zokar, watching the two young dragons frolic around them.

"Because they are not afraid of you," advised Ataar.

"Right," said Zokar dubiously, wondering why the adult dragons would be afraid of him. He stared at the young dragons. They stood about twice his height, and were covered in tough-looking grey scales that were shot through with shimmering crystalline colours of purple and black. Their wings were leathery and shiny purple, and their heads looked a little like a cross between the heads of the alligators and horses that Zokar had seen on Earth. Their eyes were huge, green, with catlike vertical slits. When threatened or frightened, they faded into invisibility within seconds.

"How do they do that?" Zokar asked Ataar, "Go invisible like that?"

Ataar smiled, "They don't. They're just babies, they can't cross the planes without help from their parents. They just make you stop seeing them."

"It's some sort of telepathic manipulation? They must be very powerful to affect elves telepathically?" asked Zokar.

"Exactly," agreed Ataar, "Handy for them."

"Yes, just in case cooking people is an ineffective deterrent, I suppose," agreed Zokar wryly.

Chapter Thirty-four

Zokar awoke two mornings later, alone, pressed up against a rock, his body curled into a sleeping ball on the only short grass around, in the shade and shelter between three rocks. He peered out through a gap between the rocks, then sighed with relief as he saw what had awoken him; a shuttle, landed only thirty metres away on the knoll. There was no sign of the dragons, Shiva or his father. Throughout the last two nights the horizon all around him had been lit by lightning flashes and red fires. The distant crack and boom of battle had been a constant accompaniment to his dreams. At one stage he had watched a huge ship burn down through the atmosphere, disintegrating as it went, until what was left of it crashed and imploded about five miles away. Zokar, a wise campaigner, had seen the huge flash and ducked behind a huge rock and counted seven seconds until the crack of the explosion flattened the grass on the knoll and took out a few dead or weak trees around his position.

To his immense relief, the figure that stepped out of the shuttle after the obligatory security detail in their golden armour, was a familiar one; Laura St James.

She walked slowly over to Zokar, and asked, "Fancy a coffee, Zokar?"

He stared at her white face, her slow gait, and the deep circles around her eyes, then nodded and led her to the fireplace that he had made two nights before. She glanced at it and the flames roared back into life from the coals, and Zokar put a frame over the fire and hung two coffee mugs from it.

He waited as long as he could, then asked, "Shiva?"

"Is alive and well, as is your father," she answered quickly, mercifully. He nodded gratefully. It was as close as Zokar would ever allow himself to come to showing concern for others in front of a human, or part human. He asked quietly, "Who died?"

"Mikey and his friends, and a few other good ones," she sighed, "And one of your dragon friends, Vulcana."

"No," whispered Zokar, closing his eyes.

"Pyrrhus went mad after that. He and Shiva killed, oh," she shook her head, "Millions of bugs, I think. Did you see the sky burning?"

"Yes. I thought for a while the whole atmosphere would be burnt away."

"No," she said distantly, "There was a way to stop that," but she looked shaken, and Zokar realized and asked her, "You stopped that from happening?"

"I had to. It is Atlantis, after all," she sighed, and swayed.

"You're exhausted," he noticed, and looked at the shuttle.

"Yes. Shiva was-" she stopped and stared into the fire. Zokar stirred and handed her the coffee, and then took his and sipped, until she looked up at him, "Did you know what he was like, Zokar? Do you know what he is?"

"A warrior? People forget, he is so gentle."

"I don't know. God help him, Zokar. There was no real way to be discriminate in what he was destroying. He would go for the Bugs, but there was a lot, an awful lot of collateral damage."

"You fixed what you could?"

"I couldn't keep up with him!" she exclaimed, distraught, "He's too powerful. Not even my powers were enough to contain the damage that he did. We lost a lot of innocents. I suppose they would have died anyway, slowly and more painfully, had the Bugs taken Atlantis."

"Powerful?" asked Zokar, puzzled. "Shiva, too powerful for you?"

There was a long silence, but Laura did not answer him. Zokar asked, "What now?"

"He's asking for you, Zokar."

Zokar nodded, and stood up, holding a hand out to help her up. She looked weak, only human, for the first time since he had met her. Her powers had been drained over the last few days, and by Shiva. Quiet, innocuous Shiva, who would not even destroy a hideous Gentrakian if he could help it. The gentlest warrior that Zokar had ever known. Zokar sincerely hoped Shiva would not remember all that had happened over the last two days. Perhaps "crossing the planes" to fight with the dragons would not allow Shiva to remember much. He wondered what he could do to help his friend, if Shiva did remember.

But Laura looked up at him and managed a weak smile, "I'm glad Atlantis survived." Zokar nodded gravely, and she continued, "I'm glad you're okay."

"Thank you."

She shook her head, and continued, "Because I don't know what the hell anyone could have done to stop Shiva, if you had been killed."

Zokar said wryly, "At least he is concerned for my welfare."

"Many are, Zokar, you'd be surprised."

"Who?"

"Trudi for one. Your father, Arlene, Nick, Karl, the crew of the Reingold."

"Don't stretch yourself," laughed Zokar, stopping her, "Now you're just making up names."

They walked on, and arrived back at the shuttle.

"You didn't mention Dom," said Zokar.

"Why should she?" asked a deep voice, and Zokar looked up in surprise to see Dom poke his head out of the shuttle.

"I should blast you," sighed Zokar, "But I am too tired."

"Ah, Zokar, charming as ever," smiled Dom, and

glanced at Laura.

"What are you doing here?" Zokar asked him sourly.

Dom was silent for a moment, then admitted, "I thought my sister could use some backup for a while. Shiva's a bit of a loose cannon at the moment."

Zokar raised his eyebrows, "Shiva is no danger to her."

"No," said Dom firmly, surprising Zokar, "He is no danger to you. To everyone else, he is a danger."

"He's as human as you Keallachs!" snapped Zokar, but Dom countered.

"That's not saying much. Besides, you didn't see him in action. Laura and I did."

Zokar looked from one face to the other, and realized that Dom looked as exhausted as Laura, "It took both of you to control him?"

"We didn't control him. We were just running damage control behind him," admitted Dom.

"Let's go talk to him," said Zokar

"Arlene's on her way over. There's to be a big ceremony," said Laura tiredly, looking less than thrilled at the prospect.

"Where?"

"The Halls of Atlantis."

Zokar nodded, and the shuttle hummed into life as the last of the gold-armoured guards boarded behind them.

Chapter Thirty-five

Shiva didn't look like an unstoppable destructive power. He looked like a captain without his ship. Like an exhausted and too-human merchant spaceman, a little lost without his elvish First Officer. Zokar approached him in the palace of Atlantis, picking his way through the clean-up crews. The damage here hadn't been too bad. Zokar had flown over much countryside and half the city to get to the palace, however, and had seen the fields ripped down to bedrock, the blazing streets, the shattered buildings. The bodies.

Zokar walked up beside him and studied the powerful but bent figure. Shiva looked as defeated as Zokar had ever seen him, and he could have been described as huddled, if he weren't so huge and imposing as to make it difficult to huddle. He was sitting with his head in both hands, and Zokar said quietly, "Shiva."

"Zokar!" exclaimed Shiva, and jumped up. Zokar noticed a slight tremble in Shiva's legs at the sudden movement, though, and reached out a hand to steady Shiva by an elbow. The human, to his surprise, stepped forward and embraced him awkwardly in a fierce bear hug, "I wasn't sure you had survived."

"I had the common sense to stay where my father told me to stay. I figured you would all try avoiding the destruction of that particular knoll."

"Ye-yes, of course," agreed Shiva, smiling now.

"Come, sit back down. Tell me what happened," said Zokar, and they sat and began to talk.

It was hours later that Zokar and Shiva noticed a stir

and a hush in the crowd, and saw a group of gold-suited warriors approaching them. Behind the royal guards walked a group of deadly looking young elvish women, in gold armour that wound snake-like around their bodies, over a sheer white fabric shot with gold, which they wore under their gold armour. Their arms were encircled from wrists to shoulders in the same gold snake-like armour, with streams of the white and gold fabric descending from the arms to the floor. Their legs were clad similarly, but with shorter trails of cloth. At the neck, the gold snake motifs took a loop upwards at each side of their neck, in just the right position to protect them from a knife to the carotid artery, Zokar noted with interest. Each of them carried an ornate gold bow and arrows, and either daggers or swords or small nunchuck-like devices, and a disruptor at each hip.

"The Royal Guard," observed Zokar.

Behind them, two figures in spectacular outfits followed. Shiva realised with a shock that it was Dom and Laura. Laura wore a flowing blue dress shot with white and gold and green, reminiscent of the colours of Earth seen from space, a deep blue cap and over that an elaborate snake-like headdress of pure white, that looked like some sort of metal, with a peculiar sheen. Dom was dressed in formal black robes, similarly flowing, which were flecked throughout with blue and red strings of indecently large jewels. On his head he wore a black helmet with deep royal blue wings sprouting from its surface. They looked every bit the royalty that Zokar had always known they were.

"Shiva, Zokar," said Laura, "Time to get decked out for the victory ceremony."

Zokar raised his eyes but stayed by Shiva's side as they were led away. Shiva looked sideways and grinned at Laura, "What?" she demanded, seeing his look.

"That outfit's bigger than you," he chuckled and she raised an arch eyebrow, and countered with, "Wait til you see what you're wearing!"

Shiva shivered a little and glanced at Zokar, who

raised his eyes to the ceiling again. Laura and Dom showed Shiva and Zokar to some huge, white marble rooms that had survived the destruction, and left them, going off to find Arlene.

Shiva and Zokar entered a room full of clothing with a fussy old couple who ran about in a surprisingly sprightly manner which belied their years, excitedly collecting first one set of golden armour, then another, for Shiva, until they were both happy with a mixed gold and white one. They quickly cleaned and polished it using a high-tech cleaning enclosure that looked like a small wardrobe but flashed and glowed for a few seconds before opening up and revealing the now gleaming outfit.

Zokar rolled his eyes when he looked at Shiva. The human was dressed in the armour, and a white ceremonial robe that was both underneath the armour and integrated with it, "Just like those girls we saw earlier," teased Zokar. On top of Shiva's head was a similar helmet to the one Dom wore, except that it was white, and instead of wings like Dom's helmet, had a golden lightning bolt coiled around it that morphed into two snakes, one white and one gold, atop the helmet. The snakes twined around each other to form a point to the helmet. Down Shiva's arms, two snakes made of gold made up the armour, until they reached his wrists where the snakes once more morphed into lightning bolts, arching up from his forearms and over his wrists to curve protectively over the top of his hands and protect them from sword wounds. The rest of his armour was gold with white snakes and lightning bolts in various configurations conforming to his muscular torso. Zokar noted with approval that Shiva's costume had the same familiar loop over the carotid artery as he had seen on the other costumes. Knives were a favourite weapon among Elves, and their armour reflected this, protecting the neck, wrists, lower back and under the arms particularly. The ceremony they were attending was strictly speaking a Galactic Union affair, but the only ceremonial clothes available were Elvish, except of course for what

Arlene and Ataar had brought with them on their ship.

Zokar smugly donned his simple black armour and declined a helmet. He looked spectacular in the black armour, with his silver eyes and hair and great height, and provided a contrast to the ornate costumes of the others. He did accept a black bow and arrows and a large black sword, however, which attracted Shiva's interest, "What's it made of?"

"Black titanium," offered Zokar, and swung it with a look of familiarity. Ataar met them and told them they were due in the main auditorium in five minutes. Ataar too, was dressed in simple black warrior clothes and armour, and Shiva stared at the two of them, then commented, "You look more like brothers than father and son."

"Come," said Ataar, his eyes happy to see them, but containing an undertone of lingering sadness that Zokar guessed was due to the death of Vulcana, and other companions that Zokar would be told the names of later. They left for the great hall, Shiva stopping first to thank the old couple who had outfitted them, who stood with hands clasped ecstatically, watching them go.

"What's with them?" asked Shiva.

"Oh, it's been a while, I guess, since they've had something like this to do," observed Zokar.

They made their way to the auditorium, and Shiva caught his first glimpse of Arlene in person.

"She's tiny!" he exclaimed to Zokar, and Ataar nudged him, "Don't judge a book by its cover."

Arlene was indeed, dwarfed by the peacock-like white, blue and gold costume that seemed to engulf her so that she was a tiny form, like a small dark ant trapped in a bowl of confectionery.

She waited for the music to stop and the group that Shiva and Zokar were in to halt before her, before beginning a long speech. On her right side stood Dom, and at her left Laura, both looking like haughty, remote statues. Zokar caught Shiva's eyes and noticed that his captain, who would

171

stride onto a battlefield with blaster fire lighting up the air around his ears, without a blink, looked nervous. Zokar smiled to himself. He had grown up surrounded by ceremony in these vast halls, and was not fazed at all. Shiva's upbringing, Zokar knew, had been very different. Zokar paid attention to the lengthly speech that Arlene had somehow found time to prepare. He was aware of Shiva gazing in amazement around them, and the human whispered, "How did they do any of this, the clean-up alone, let alone the music, organizing the ceremony, the speech. It's amazing that you Elves have achieved this much in so little time. All this in a city, and on a planet, devastated by the worst, hardest-fought, battle in Elvish history."

Zokar whispered, "Hush," and Shiva subsided into silence.

The droning voice of Arlene slowed down, and Shiva looked up sharply at the podium as she said, "And so, Shiva Kiran, the planet Atlantis and indeed the Galactic Union is deeply indebted to you for your part in resolving this conflict. In view of this, I invite you to ask for a reward for your services rendered to both."

Zokar could feel the startled jolt in Shiva's body, then the human's face went very still. Zokar was not overly surprised when Shiva, instead of giving the expected reaction of politely declining the Empress's offer, spoke up. "Actually, Oh Most High, there is something I would like you to give me in exchange for my efforts."

Arlene stared at him, her expression unreadable.

Shiva took a deep breath, and went on, with Zokar and Ataar staring open-mouthed at him now, forgetting that they were Elves and should look dignified at all times. Shiva said, "I'd like you to give me the star system of Sol, including the planet Earth."

Zokar felt the breath leave his body at the sheer audacity of the request.

Arlene froze. It was the last request she had expected from the soft-eyed human. "Earth is not mine to give. It belongs to the Greys."

"Then buy it back from them." His lapis blue eyes were challenging, "You have the money."

She sat back, managing after all to move within her tent of ceremonial robes and said, "You know, I wasn't sure what to make of you at first. But I am starting to think that my daughter has chosen wisely." Laura, standing next to her, looked like she was trying not to grin. Trudi, in the group behind Laura, was biting her lip too.

There was a long silence, then Arlene said, "Very well. But what if the Greys will not sell it back to me?"

"Then I will change my request and ask for a battle fleet of five thousand vessels, and ask the elves to man them for me," declared Shiva, his blue eyes steady, "And then I will get the Greys to change their minds about selling Earth back, or I will kill every last one of them."

Arlene smiled stiffly, and said, "As you wish. Sol and its planets are yours, Shiva Kiran."

Ataar shook his head, and Zokar whispered to Shiva, "The arse. The sheer, unadulterated arse of you!" Shiva grinned happily back.

The music came back on and they were ushered out of the hall into a banquet area. Zokar realized just how hungry he was. To Zokar's surprise, he and Shiva were seated at the same table as the Empress. Arlene did not look happy, Zokar noticed, and assumed she was irritated by Shiva claiming the Solar system and Earth from her.

But as the night wore on and Arlene looked less and less happy, Zokar noticed a stream of couriers going to and from their table, stopping to talk to Arlene in low, urgent tones.

Eventually, after one courier had been quizzed thoroughly, Arlene stood up suddenly. The whole banquet hall crowd rose to its feet as one. Arlene whispered something to Ataar and then left with him and Dom at her side.

"What is it? What's happening?" asked Shiva.

Laura walked slowly over to him, and asked, "When are we leaving for Earth, Shiva?"

Shiva flung down his napkin and collected Zokar with a look, "Now, I think, would be as good a time as any."

Zokar muttered something, and Shiva said, "What?"

"I don't know who has more gall, Domhan Keallach for selling Earth, or you for asking the Empress to buy it back for you."

"It's only a star system, Zokar," Laura pointed out.

Zokar stared at her and shook his head, "Only a Terran, or a Keallach, could think like that."

Chapter Thirty-six

They took several of the Opal ships and headed back towards Earth. It was one thing to have legal ownership of Earth, Shiva and Zokar knew. It was another thing to take it back off the Greys. Possession is nine-tenths of the law.

Laura walked into the room and glanced at the main mess's viewer, which showed the depressing view of the cloud of Grey ships still surrounding the Earth.

"What's up, Tru?" asked Laura, coming up to the table where Trudi sat looking pensive, staring at the viewer, ignoring Gan who was happily batting Ghrian's flicking tail as he munched on a huge bone that the chef had found for him.

Trudi shook herself out of her reverie, and said, "Oh, just thinking about humans."

"What about you?" teased Laura.

"Oh, it's just that, the bugs want our bodies, the Greys want our minds: I never really thought of us as... fodder, before," said Trudi.

"Oh, thanks, neither had I. What a lovely thought to carry around with me from now on," grumbled Laura.

Trudi shivered, "It's not funny, Lor. They're parasites, all of them. Parasites. They're disgusting. Yech. Remember on the farm when we had to drench all the horses for worms?"

Laura frowned, "Yep, I remember. Dad said it was like chemical warfare. Only not really, because the chemicals only harmed the worms, not the horses."

They sat in silence for a few moments, then Laura looked up at Trudi and said, "Are you thinking what I'm

175

thinking, Trudi?"

"I don't know. What I'm thinking is that, we've been so tied up in the fact that these Greys are mental parasites, that we keep forgetting their physical limitations. And the fact that they are on a planet which is not their home planet. Remember the Fey? How only four survived, out of twenty that crashed?" said Trudi.

"Hmmm. If we could think of something that was harmful to Greys, but not to humans?" but then Laura stopped and sighed, "What am I saying?"

"What's wrong?" asked Trudi.

Laura sighed again and looked down, then said sadly, "How many more creatures must I kill, Trudi? I don't want to kill any more. Not on this sort of scale. Shiva's right: there must be a better way."

A soft voice from behind her surprised both Laura and Trudi. Shiva leaned down and kissed Laura softly on the top of the head, and said softly, "Well, what do you know? It's not every day you see a conscience being born."

Laura turned to him and gave him a sort of half-frown, half-smile, but said nothing. Trudi fell silent, and then said, "Laura did what she had to do, Shiva. There was no time to muck around. They were going to blow up our planet."

Shiva nodded, and said, "But this time we have time. And we will use it. These Greys: they are not particularly violent by nature, and I have a feeling that there must be some other way of getting rid of them."

Zokar had arrived with Shiva, and stood silently behind him, listening intently to the conversation, head tilted, like a small child trying to comprehend higher mathematics. He found talk of consciences confusing and mildly disturbing, because he strongly suspected that he simply did not possess one. He wisely remained silent, but sat next to Trudi and gave her a tiny smile, all he ever allowed himself in public. Trudi leaned over and kissed him on the cheek, but he stared at the menu pad on the table and did not respond.

Laura noticed Zokar's reaction to Trudi's kiss and giggled, "It's the warmth. That's why everybody loves him, isn't it Shiva?"

Shiva chuckled and pulled a chair around to sit behind Laura, straddling the chair and putting his arms around her shoulders, kissing her hand when she lifted it to his.

Zokar rolled his eyes at Shiva and Trudi and said in a tone of amused contempt, "So human."

Trudi opened her mouth to protest, but caught the slight upwards quirk in the elf's mouth, smiled and said nothing.

"Well, my friends, how do you get rid of a parasite infestation without harming the parasites?"

"I don't see why we can't just blow them all up," grumbled Zokar.

"There are practical considerations, Zokar. Fallout, both radioactive and physical, from so many ships in orbit being instantly disintegrated into floating debris. We don't want to incapacitate our human friends on Earth."

"Shiva, you're starting to sound elvish. What about not wanting to hurt the Greys?" asked Trudi, reproachfully.

"Why shouldn't we want to hurt the Greys?" asked Shiva.

"You've been hanging around these two for too long," said Trudi, nodding at Zokar and Laura, who both looked a little affronted.

Shiva glanced ruefully at Zokar and stroked Laura's hair, then asked Trudi, "What else can we do to make the Greys leave Earth? We'll have to scare them off, at the very least."

"We could just *ask* them to leave," suggested Trudi.

Zokar laughed at her, which made her blush, but she continued, "Well, has anyone thought to ask them why they left their own galaxy in the first place? Did they leave voluntarily or were they driven out?"

Everyone looked embarrassed.

"I guess we didn't," decided Shiva.

"Are you serious?" asked Zokar, staring hard at Trudi, "You don't sit down with an invading army and ask them how they *feel*. You shoot their arses to kingdom come."

"But, are they an army?" asked Trudi. There was a sudden silence.

"What?" asked Laura.

"They're not that well armed," pointed out Trudi, "I mean, considering the level of technology they must have to develop the propulsion techniques they used to get here across the Void from the Andromeda galaxy, their weapons are really... well, pretty pathetic. Not much better than ours, in fact."

"So, what are you saying?" asked Laura, "If they're not an army, what are they?"

Trudi looked down at her plate, then looked up at them all and suggested, "Refugees?"

Zokar rubbed his forehead. Humans gave him a headache, sometimes, "Are you seriously suggesting that we go off to the Grey leaders, and say, 'Hey, can we have your life story, because we think we may have got you all wrong'?"

"Yeah, pretty much," decided Trudi, "That's about what I had in mind."

"Off you go then," chuckled Zokar, and was surprised when she stood up, and Shiva with her. Shiva shrugged at Laura and Zokar and walked after Trudi. After a moment's hesitation, Zokar and Laura jumped up and followed the two humans, followed by the big cats, who had to dodge the chairs that Zokar and Laura had flung down in their haste to leave.

Two hours later, after a lengthly discussion with the Grey leaders, Shiva sat down in his chair and waved a hand at the communications officer, who cut the connection. He swung around and stared at Trudi.

"How did you know?" he asked, shaking his head.

She sighed, "I was a police officer, remember? I was trained to investigate a situation with my eyes open and not jump to conclusions. It was the lack of weaponry, and the peaceful nature of the Greys. They could have just stuffed the humans they had drained out an airlock, but they didn't, they took the trouble to put them back unharmed on Earth."

Zokar summarised, "So, there are Bugs in the Andromeda galaxy too? And they wiped out all the humans in the Grey's sector? That's not good."

"As far as the Greys know, the humans are *all* gone," said Shiva, "The Greys and the humans coexisted quite peacefully there for millennia, but when the Bugs arrived and started harvesting the humans, the Greys were basically starved out. They aren't fighters. Trudi was right about that: weaponry is a relatively new concept to them. The Greys that have arrived here were forced out to the edge of their galaxy, then they fled across the Void. When they found Earth, they set up a base outside the galactic rim and were happy to survive quietly and unnoticed out there and harvest humans on a sort of catch-and-release program. The suppression generator kept other ships away from the area, and the Union didn't know they were there, because the Union simply didn't look. But then the Bugs in Andromeda wiped out the last of the humans and the Grey refugees started arriving en masse at their base, and they had to move in on Earth. When the suppression generator was destroyed they were happy to be our allies, but when the Galactic Union and Earth started fighting, the Greys decided that they had to abandon their pacifist ways and gain a foothold in this new galaxy."

"So out in the Void, they had no home, no sunshine," pondered Trudi. Zokar frowned at her, screwing up his face, trying to keep up with the quick flow of emotions in her face and voice and failing miserably, "And then we pretty much wrecked their base when we rescued Dom."

"Yes," said Shiva, "Thus making it an imperative that they move in on Earth. When Dom offered to sell them the

Solar system and make them legitimate Galactic Union citizens, they jumped at the chance. They finally had a home again, after hundreds of years without."

"Damn," whispered Laura.

"What?" asked Zokar.

"Well, don't you see, Zokar, if we kick them out now, it would be like kicking puppies."

"I do not understand," said Zokar, "What is a puppy, and why is kicking one, like fighting an alien?"

Shiva smiled as Laura started to explain, but he looked thoughtful. He turned to the others, "Do you think Dom had all this information when he sold them Earth?"

"He could have," agreed Laura, "It would explain his actions."

Shiva asked, "Then why didn't he just tell us that?"

Trudi chuckled, "It's Dom. He never seems to feel he has to explain himself."

"Oi," Laura defended her twin.

"That doesn't solve our problem," sighed Shiva, twiddling Gan's tail tip in his hands as Gan flicked it back and forward playfully.

"What?" asked Zokar.

"Well, who among you feels like explaining to the Terrans that their planet has been sold by the Galactic Union to the Greys and that now we've decided that even though we have the resources, we may decide to leave the Greys there and won't be buying Earth back for them?"

Zokar pouted thoughtfully, "Not me."

"Sir!" the helmsman was looking incredulously at Earth, and the others turned to look.

"What's happening?" asked Trudi.

"Are they moving out?" asked Zokar, gazing at the cloud of ships around Earth as they began to form into a group away from the blue planet.

Shiva stared at the ships, and hit his communications button, "Admiral Zeeve? Sir, what's happening? Are you leaving Earth?"

The Grey admiral appeared on the main view screen, and said, "Captain Kiran, we have reviewed the information from our discussion with you, and we are most concerned about the Bug infestation which you say is threatening your galactic Core."

"Why is that your concern, sir?"

"Captain, we are familiar with the pattern of Bug infestation in a galaxy: tragically familiar. We believe that the situation in your galaxy is far more serious than you realise. We have reviewed our past actions and compared them to yours, and realised that the pacifist approach is untenable in this situation. We are therefore going to the Core to assist your Galactic Union to eliminate the Bugs from this galaxy before it is too late."

Shiva blinked and stared dumbly at the view screen, which remained on the Admiral for a few more seconds then blinked out.

Zokar said quietly, as they watched the grey ships depart, "Well, I'll be damned. It worked. Trudi's idea of talking with them actually worked."

"And you thought I was only good at blowing things up," smiled Trudi, looking smug.

"You just mobilized an entire pacifist species to war," Zokar pointed out, proudly. Trudi shook her head at him sadly, and Zokar looked even more puzzled.

"Look, there's the Reingold!" exclaimed Laura, pointing as the great vessel, in close orbit around Earth, but no longer obscured by the cloud of grey ships, emerged slowly around the curvature of the Earth into their view.

"What do we do now?" asked Zokar.

"We can't leave Earth undefended," said Laura.

"No, but there's a war brewing, and there's more at stake now than just Earth," said Shiva, looking at Laura, "There's your mother and brother, remember? We should be there, fighting with them."

"And somebody needs to tell the Union that the Greys have switched sides again," said Laura.

"Have they? Or were they just trying to survive, all along?" asked Trudi.

"Good point. Perhaps they are more like the Terrans than we realised," said Shiva. He worried his bottom lip with his teeth, "But do we take the Reingold, or go back in these blue ships? The Reingold has the range, but she's not quick enough in a fight. The Opal ships are fast, but will they have the range to even get us to the battle lines?"

"You can fit sixteen of the Opal ships in the Reingold's hold," said Trudi promptly, "That will give us the range of the Reingold, and the strike speed of the Opal ships. Once we reach the Core we can release the Opal ships to fight."

Shiva turned to her, his eyes lighting up, "That's a great idea! Why didn't I think of that?"

"It's not new. It's just like an aircraft carrier," said Trudi, "The Opal ships don't quite have the range the Reingold does, but they won't use fuel on the long journey, so they'll still be fully fuelled up and ready for the battle when we arrive. That leaves sixty-four Opal ships to defend Earth, which should be enough considering that the Union probably won't attack Earth now."

Zokar smiled.

Shiva was already moving, "Let's go home," he grinned, and headed for the bridge. They hailed the Reingold, and to their surprise found McCosker manning the bridge.

"Zokar, Shiva!" what the devil is going on? What did you say to those Greys? They just up and left!"

"Let's go, General, we have a galaxy to defend," said Shiva, "Stop and pick up fifteen Opal ships, then follow those Greys and pick us up on the way through."

The Reingold quickly did as directed, scooping up small groups of Opal ships into its massive hold, until there were fifteen ships packed in. Then it picked up the Opal ship Zokar and Shiva were on.

Shiva waited impatiently while their ship manoeuvred

at a snail's pace inside the Reingold's familiar hold, then locked onto an airlock station within the huge vessel. He stepped into the corridors of the Reingold and strode along, Zokar and the big cats right behind him.

Once back on the bridge of the Reingold, Shiva settled in his familiar central chair and looked up at Zokar and Ataar, manning the science consoles, "Full power to hypercrive."

"Aye sir," said Zokar, and the Reingold glowed for several long seconds, turned its nose towards the Core, steadied, then dived into the howling wormhole, its hold slithering with sleek, glossy Opal ships, packed like royal blue sardines into the huge empty space inside the space door. The ships were flexible, and conformed to one another, their hulls pressed tightly together in places, with tractor fields holding the whole mass together and motionless within the Reingold, so that they did not affect the movements of the huge ship.

Chapter Thirty-seven

"Where are we?" asked Laura sleepily as she arrived on the bridge of the Reingold and looked at an unfamiliar and dense starscape.

"About a thousand light years out from the Core," Shiva told her, his hand clasping hers briefly but his eyes remaining on the view screen and his scanners.

She noticed and asked, "Are we expecting hostilities?"

There should be more Comm chatter," observed Shiva, strangely tense.

Zokar glanced over at him, but only for a moment. He too, was worried by the lack of communications chatter on his console, and he had been channelling power into a comprehensive long range scan for hours now, concentrating on the galactic plane, but still covering all four dimensions.

But sometimes it was the lack of information that told more than information itself. Zokar waited for twenty-two more seconds, then announced, "Captain, we have entered the Core Zone of the Galactic Union."

"No challenge from the Border defences?" asked Shiva, not looking surprised.

"No Sir."

Zokar was not surprised by the next command, "Go to silent running status."

Elesk's voice sounded beside Zokar, small and worried, "Scanning Bug ships sir. Numbers…. It's a full swarm, sir. Numbers not ascertainable from scanners."

Zokar looked up and saw Shiva swallow as the golden haze of a vast number of Bug ships came onto their view screen.

"Looks like our work is not finished yet, Captain." Zokar tapped his console and Elesk moved over to attend the main science console. He waited for an aide to take her post, then stepped down to listen to Shiva.

"Let's see if we can run interference on these ships, give the Greys a few openings," suggested Shiva quietly. "We'll stay in silent running mode and do as much damage as we can."

"That's a dangerous approach," said Zokar. "We are unlikely to survive."

"It's where we can do the most good," muttered Shiva.

Zokar shook his head and stepped away back up to his science console, shuffling Elesk and the aide back to their positions.

It was going to be a long war. Zokar checked their supplies.

Chapter Thirty-eight

The Greys fought well, considering that it took them a few weeks to realize there was no point trying to rescue the humans stored on the Bug ships. The Bugs, when their ships were disabled, would simply disperse into space, releasing the atmosphere from the ships to help them disperse. The fact that this caused the comatose humans trapped in the disabled ships to perish was not a concern to the Bugs.

Many Grey ships were destroyed when they slowed down to attempt to assist the humans, and for a while it looked like the Greys would all be destroyed. But after a few weeks, the Greys apparently put their minds to improving their weaponry, and began destroying the Bug ships en masse with some sort of dark matter wormhole device.

The battle continued, with the Reingold like a deadly ghost hovering around and doing as much damage as possible to the Bug ships as possible.

After a few weeks, the Reingold was running low on fuel, and low on supplies.

Zokar scanned the area around the Reingold once more. He was hungry and irritable. The numbers of Grey ships had been reduced to a pathetic few. The up side of that was that the Bug ships seemed just as scarce.

Then Zokar saw it. A cloud of gold, growing like an expanding balloon on his screen. He hit the comm button, "Captain to the Bridge. Incoming Bug flotilla... massive."

Shiva arrived in less than thirty seconds, still pulling his uniform on. He looked over Zokar's shoulder, and stared at the screen for a long time.

Then he looked at Zokar and said, "Set course back

for the Core."

"We're going to run away?" Zokar's voice was edgy.

"Got any other suggestions?"

Zokar stared at the cloud on his sensor screen, then sighed. "No. There is nothing we can do."

They quietly plotted a course around the invading Bug swarm and set course for the Core.

Zokar looked up into Shiva's blue eyes, which looked desperate for the first time since Zokar had met his captain. Zokar pursed his lips, "Shiva, what can we possibly do, against an invading force of this magnitude?"

Shiva frowned. "We cannot defend the galaxy. All we can do is defend the Core."

"The Core Planet?"

"If that's all we can do, Zokar, then that's what we will do."

"What if we can't do that, Shiva?"

There was a long silence. "Then we will die," sighed Shiva.

They were not the only ones with the same idea. From all around the galaxy, ships and flotillas and whole fleets appeared around them as they made way towards the Core planet. Most moved at breakneck speed. There were a few desperate messages requesting supplies, and over Zokar's objections, every time Shiva said, "Yes." Several times they stopped to take disabled wrecks into their shuttle bay, rescue the occupants and eject the remains of the ruined star ships. The complement of the Reingold had doubled by the time they came into sensor range of the Core planet.

Zokar grew more and more reticent as he pondered the gravity of their situation. They were low on fuel, low on ammunition and supplies, and even if they reached the Core planet they were unlikely to be of any assistance in the defence effort. The most likely end to their lives would be that the Bugs would overrun the Reingold and put the humans into storage on their ships. Zokar, useless to the Bugs for food, would be tossed out an airlock.

He sighed and looked at his scanners. The gold cloud had expanded behind them so that Zokar could still see it on his scanners. Zokar squinted as one edge of the cloud shifted, then seemed to turn blue.

Zokar looked closer at his scanner, and said suddenly, "Captain!"

"What?" Shiva's mein changed instantly in response to Zokar's tone.

"Sir," said Zokar and turned with a broad smile, "It's the Humans."

"What?"

"The Terrans."

Shiva was up at the scanners in three bounds, and Zokar leaned back to allow him to watch as the blue cloud began to eat steadily into the gold cloud.

"How many ships do the Terrans have?" wondered Shiva.

"As many as they could build in three months, it would appear. They must have been building them somewhere out of the solar system while the war was going on. Trust the Terrans."

"Er... Zokar." Shiva was heading back for the command chair, waving at the scanner.

Zokar looked back at his scanner, "The Bugs are retreating. Oh."

"Yeah, they're retreating right back down our throats! Battle stations!"

"Why would they retreat to the Core?" asked Zokar, puzzled, "Why not disperse?"

"I don't know, but we have another planet to defend!" said Shiva.

And defend the Core planet they did. With the help of Laura and eventually Dom, the flow of Bugs was destroyed, and Arlene's gratitude was such that she awarded the Terrans the position of First Fleet, and Laura St James sovereignty over the Solar system and a thousand light years in all directions.

For Shiva's role in protecting the Core planet and assisting with the humanitarian efforts afterwards, the Reingold and its crew were invited to a special ceremony on Atlantis.

Chapter Thirty-nine

Zokar's elvish ears picked up the sound, where no human would have heard it; the steady, rhythmic beat hovered erratically just on the edge of elvish hearing. He went into Shiva's cabin and found Shiva sitting on his bed in his cabin, feet crossed at his ankles, tapping steadily on a small drum held upright between his knees, eyes closed.

"Something is troubling you," Zokar hazarded. He was slowly learning about emotions. Although, he was doing it mathematically; he had correlated in his mind the incidence of drum playing by his captain with the incidence of Shiva being in a depressed emotional state. The correlation to date had been very high, so Zokar was fairly confident of his assessment of Shiva's state of mind. However he was puzzled; the battle had been fought, the war won. Why would Shiva be troubled now?

Shiva's hands stilled on the drum, and the noise stopped, leaving the silence to echo between them. Then he spoke softly, but his voice was haunted as he finally looked up at Zokar, "What am I? What am I, Zokar, in these times that I forget? Do you know? Have you seen?"

"Not really," Zokar lied, because he did not think that Shiva could stand to hear the truth. Not gentle, human Shiva who killed only when necessary and spoke the language of feelings and consciences as easily as Zokar integrated multi-dimensional mathematical arrays. Shiva was a warrior, yes, but he fought by his own set of inviolable ethical rules, and some instinct in Zokar told him that to know the true nature and extent of his destructive abilities would in turn, destroy Shiva.

"You're lying. To protect me? How bad do I get?" demanded Shiva, and rested his chin on his hands, looking up into Zokar's eyes, waiting for an answer. When Zokar took too long to reply, Shiva sank his face into his hands.

Zokar knelt down in front of the man who had become his friend, and because Shiva had pulled Zokar back from the edge of despair many years ago and taught him to care again, even if Zokar was not that good at it yet, the big elf pulled Shiva's hands gently off his face and lied again as the blue eyes looked up to meet his reluctantly, "Shiva, you were in a war zone. The dragons and the Bugs did the real damage. You were just in the wrong place at the wrong time. We all were. Don't overthink it. Every time you were... called to help, it was for the better. The change was for the better."

Shiva sighed, and said, "I guess you're right." He looked up at Zokar, and stood up, "You're a good friend, you know that, Zokar?"

"No," demurred Zokar, his eyes troubled, "Not good. As good as I can be, but I'm still just an elf."

A thought struck Shiva, "You don't think I'd be a danger to you, do you?"

Zokar smiled and remembered a lone figure striding down the ruined avenues of an Atlantic city, blaster fire flying from his hands like chain lightning and the fires of vengeance coming from his eyes, coming to rescue a lost friend. "No, Shiva. Never."

But Zokar stared at the view screen, looking at the dense wash of stars sitting unmoving in the small rectangle, and wondered just how long it would be before the wanderlust in Shiva lured him away from the Core and away from Laura; out into the distant reaches of the Galaxy again with Zokar. Zokar hoped it wasn't too long. The elf smiled.

Chapter Forty

"Another ceremony," groaned Shiva, "Do they do anything else in here?"

"At least we are alive to see it," Zokar pointed out dryly, his eyes amused as they met Shiva's.

Shiva smiled, "True, but I swear these costumes weigh more every time they redesign them."

"Perhaps they are trying to slow you down, my friend," chuckled Zokar warmly.

Shiva said nothing, but smiled quietly to himself, ducking his face away so that Zokar would not see the embarrassing warmth in his blue eyes. Zokar had, for the first time in Shiva's recall, just called him 'friend.'

They strode into the Great Hall. Shiva grumbled, "I can't even see them."

Laura and Trudi were waiting for them just inside the entrance, and Laura heard Shiva's comment. She smiled and pointed out, "That's because they're a thousand metres away, silly."

Then the crowd spotted them emerging into the hall and a wall of sound hit them as the crowd cheered, making all conversation impossible. Shiva and Zokar waited for it to die down as they walked up the aisle, but it continued, getting louder.

Zokar grimaced. Now he knew why people never dawdled up the Great Hall. The noise was so loud that it hurt his elven ears and he had to resist the urge to cover them with his hands.

Laura gazed about her, intrigued by the sheer diversity of life forms lining the aisle. Up until now she had mostly been in Terran ships or on the Reingold, fighting for her life and the continued existence of her fellow humans, or out on the Rim where few but the most intrepid of species, that is the humans, Fey and Elves, ventured. These people were civilians, from the many planets near the galactic Core, and they ranged from insectoid to reptilian, to human, to some things she just couldn't begin to classify in her mind. Eventually Trudi, Shiva and Zokar stopped beside her and she realized they had come to the open space before the dais where Arlene sat, Ataar standing solemnly beside her, Dom on her right side. Laura stopped, exchanging a rueful look with Trudi.

Arlene began, "My good friends, welcome at last to your home," and Laura felt the hackles rise on the back of her neck. Arlene was never this nice.

Arlene continued, but Laura soon tuned out the voice, her thoughts turning inward, considering for the first time in many weeks the events of the preceding months. She thought of Arlene screaming at her, of the Union fleet heading towards Earth with instructions to destroy her planet, of the many times Arlene had disbelieved them all when they told her the truth. When you exist in a world of politics and lies, thought Laura, it must be almost impossible to see when someone else is telling the truth.

Arlene's voice cut through Laura's reverie as she heard her own name mentioned, "… my daughter, Laura St James. Upon you, Laura, I confer the title of-"

Laura's voice rang out loud and clear, interrupting Arlene, and the crowd as one gasped, "Actually, Mother, don't bother."

Arlene stuttered for a few moments, then stared at Laura, her mouth open as if to say something. No sound came out. Shiva and Zokar were looking at her with great interest. The rest of the occupants of the Hall were staring at her in complete shock. Nobody had ever interrupted the Empress before. Laura smiled smugly, and continued, "You see, Mother, at this moment, the Terran forces hold the Core.

We have destroyed the Bug infestation and saved the Galactic Union's collective hide. Our forces are now strategically placed to hold the Core against all hostiles, including, if we consider them hostile, the remaining Galactic Union forces. You will confer nothing on me, Mother, because the Core is mine, and your Galactic Union fleet, if you defy me, is toast."

"This is preposterous!" gasped Arlene.

"Not really," smiled Laura, with a sudden evil grin that made the audience suck back on itself in trepidation, "Unexpected? Perhaps, although to a Terran such a course of action would seem simply... logical," she shrugged.

Zokar smiled at her admiringly. He did so like the Terran way of thinking.

"I will send our forces to destroy your insignificant little planet!" cried Arlene, "You cannot protect both at once, the Core and Earth!"

"Oh right, I didn't think of that..." said Laura, her sarcastic tone and smile belying her words, "But really, do you think you'd have any political support for that decision when the Terrans forces start razing the surfaces of the Core planets to blackened crisps? Just like you threatened to do to Earth, not so long ago?"

Arlene looked at her for many seconds, then decided, "You're bluffing. You would never do such a thing. There would be nothing left for you to rule."

"Oh, no, Mother, you obviously just don't understand us Terrans. After all, what's a few dead aliens here and there, to us?" retorted Laura, looking bored, "So we get a nice empty Galaxy all to ourselves? At least no one would be constantly threatening to blow us up!"

"Are you mad?"

"Not really, it's just that your Union has been pissing me off for months now," replied Laura calmly.

Arlene was shaking now with rage and standing up out of her throne, "I will stop you!"

"How?" asked Laura insouciantly.

Arlene looked at her, realising her position. The blue Opal ships of Terra protected the Core as they spoke. Protected it, and thereby occupied it; the controlling centre of Galactic Union territory. "What do you want?" she hissed at Laura.

Laura took in a deep breath, and her voice rang out loud and clear, "Succession."

Arlene began to laugh, "You? You want the throne of the Galactic Union? Who do you think you are?"

"Zokar, give the order to activate the Terran forces," said Laura, and Shiva turned to Zokar, "You're in on this?"

"Kill him! Kill that Elf!" roared Arlene.

Ataar cried "No!" and glared at Arlene, stepping away from her and the throne, towards the edge of the dais and closer to Zokar.

But at the same time, Laura called out, "Dead-man switch!"

Everybody froze. Arlene understood her without having to ask, and held up a hand, restraining her guards; if Laura or any of her friends died, the activation of the Terran forces would proceed anyway, under prior orders. It was exactly what Arlene would have done under the circumstances. Arlene turned slowly to glare at Ataar, "You, Ataar? You would turn on me?"

"You just ordered my son to be killed," Ataar pointed out, his voice icy as only an elf's voice can be icy.

"You will regret your treachery, Ataar," snarled Arlene just as coldly. The elf raised a cool eyebrow at her.

There was a deathly silence throughout the Hall. All eyes were on Arlene; nobody seemed to be breathing. Eventually Arlene turned to Laura, "Do you know what you are asking?"

"Yes."

"Really? Do you really want to become the queen bee at the centre of this hive?" asked Arlene. "Your life never your own, your very existence devoted to the ongoing welfare of all those around you?"

"Sounds to me," said Laura, her voice still ringing out confidently, clear and bell-like in the Great Hall, "That you've had just about enough of being Galactic Leader. I think the pressure of the job's getting a bit much for you."

Arlene was going vaguely purple, and said, "If your concern is for my welfare, then do not make me hand over the Galactic Union to you under threat."

Laura gazed intently at Arlene, and asked, "What do you want?"

"A peaceful succession will suffice," said Arlene, suddenly smiling oddly.

"Declare it then," said Laura, her voice still wary.

There was silence for a heartbeat, but Arlene was already bringing the space-time continuum to a grinding halt. The voices suddenly distorted and died around Laura, and she gazed around, staring at the frozen figures around her. She jumped as she caught movement in the periphery of her vision, and saw Arlene walking towards her.

"Relax," smiled Arlene, "Weapons do not work in stasis."

"Since when did you need weapons? Say your piece and release my friends!" growled Laura. Neither of them noticed Dom, unaffected by the stasis effect, edging carefully across the dais towards Ataar.

Arlene said, "I don't have to, you know. I could keep us like this forever. Do you think I am Empress for nothing?"

"What do you want?" asked Laura.

"Nothing that you can give. I am about to win this little chess game, my dear. You will think you have won... to some extent, but soon you will realise that you have just created a prison for yourself, for all eternity. Oh, and by the way, I am going to tear the heart out of your little group of friends. I just thought you'd like to know that. The funny thing is, I don't think you even know who I'm talking about. Oh well, no matter, just as long as you get the blame."

"What?" Laura asked.

"Oh, you'll figure it out. Perhaps when you realize what I am really capable of, you will see just what an amateur you are at all this," she turned slightly and said in a louder voice, "You can stop sneaking about, Dom, I'm certainly not going to hurt Laura."

"Who then?" demanded Laura, then said, "Don't you hurt Shiva!"

Arlene laughed, "You fool. Do you think any of us could hurt him? You have no idea who he is, do you?"

"What?" said Laura.

But then Laura felt the stasis ease around her and the voices of the crowd returned. She turned to see Zokar step towards her, then frowned as she saw the mask of terror on his face, the contortion of sinews and muscles fighting something invisible that was lifting his arms, obviously against his will. Laura suddenly saw the long ceremonial knife in his hands as he lunged towards her, his gait awkward as he fought the power that drove his hands towards her heart. His lips formed the desperate word, "Shiva!"

"Zokar, no!" cried Laura, throwing up her hands instinctively to protect herself, realizing that Arlene, who had somehow appeared back on the dais in front of her throne, was controlling the elf.

Shiva turned at Zokar's cry for help, and at Laura's protest, but he turned just in time to see two ragged bolts of destructive lightning arc from Laura's hands and hit the elf. For a fraction of second Zokar was surrounded by a buzzing white nimbus of light. Then there was a deafening crack and blinding flash around Zokar, whose single agonised cry of pain was cut short as he disappeared.

Everybody stared at the spot in the Great Hall where Zokar Rizian had stood only moments before. There was nothing there now except a smoking black mark on the floor.

Chapter Forty-one

Laura stared, horrified, at the empty place where Zokar had stood.

Shiva roared desperately, "No!"

Trudi screamed, and threw herself on the black smoking patch, clawing at it like she could somehow drag Zokar back from the melted scraps of flooring. She looked at Laura, slowly registering the horrified expression on Laura's face.

Shiva turned to Laura, shaking his head. He tried to say something, but no sound emerged, even though she could see his mouth moving, forming the soundless word, "Why?" He sank to his knees and gave a loud cry, a harsh agonised sound which tore into Laura's ears, then became louder and louder. Screams broke out around Shiva as a swirling wind started to curl around him, his eyes seemed to brighten to white and his skin slowly changed colour, glowing brighter and brighter until it was almost unbearably white. Laura and the rest of the occupants of the Great Hall were transfixed, then a crack of lightning within the Hall startled everybody. Shiva tried to stand, staggered a few steps and fell again, then, surrounded by white fire, stood.

"Is he burning up?" screamed Trudi.

Dom had reached them, towing Ataar with them, and Dom grabbed Laura. "We must stop him!"

"What's happening?" cried Laura, "Shiva!"

"Use the stasis!" Dom roared at Laura over the diabolical noise of wind and lightning that now filled the hall. Many people had been knocked to the floor, and others were trying to crawl away towards the great doors. People screamed and crawled over the top of each other to get out the narrow side doors. Even the huge entrance at the far end of the Great Hall became crowded with frightened people trying to escape.

Laura felt Dom's hand grab hers, and she tried to concentrate. Together they felt the space-time continuum shift around them, and everything began to slow down again. Trudi's voice was eerily distorted and deep as she cried out, "What are yoooouuu... dooo-?" but her lips stopped moving before she had uttered the last word.

"Christ," swore Laura, staring at the frozen crowd around them as the stasis finally took effect. She walked up to Shiva and ducked warily around a motionless lightning bolt. Dom brushed past it, and said, "It can't hurt you; there's no time, so the current cannot flow."

"Oh."

She walked around Shiva, and studied the bright white skin and glowing eyes of her lover, then looked perplexed at Dom, "What the hell is going on? What's happening to Shiva?"

Arlene's voice from behind them surprised them both, "Perhaps you should ask rather, what is Shiva becoming? Something that will keep you two occupied for quite some time, I'd imagine." She went on, almost to herself, "I had wondered where he had disappeared to."

"Mother!" growled Dom, "What did you do?"

Arlene gazed up in the sky, "Oh, sorry, dears, I forgot to warn you."

"What?" Laura felt her concentration slip, and the stasis weakened. The lightning next to her crackled into existence again, stinging her arm, "Ow!" She hastily turned her concentration back to maintaining the stasis. Dom shot her a look.

Arlene seemed quite relaxed about the situation, "You see, in chess, if you want to take a powerful piece out of the game, you lock it in with another piece, creating a stalemate which takes both pieces out of the game."

"What?" asked Dom, his eyes blazing with anger, "Mother, this isn't a game. I can't believe you just killed Zokar!"

"Oh? I did? And what are you going to do about it?" smiled Arlene.

"I'll tell you what I'm going to do about it, I'm going to-" began Dom angrily, but she hushed them both with a waggling finger.

"Darlings, neither of you can do a damn thing until you figure out how to unlock this lovely little stasis field you have both created, without releasing that creature," and she pointed at Shiva, "... on this planet, and I'm sure he'll do a damn sight better job of destroying the place than the Bugs ever did. And I don't think you'll find persuading him to stop an easy task, especially since he now thinks you, my dear Laura, just killed his friend Zokar."

"I did kill him," whispered Laura.

Arlene stared at her unreadably but said nothing. She wondered over to poke a finger at the still form of Shiva, "Both you and Dom, my dear, are loose cannons. You have no idea what it takes to run a galaxy, let alone seven of them. I'm simply taking a stronger hold on the reins of power. I have let you run for a little while, children, but now it's time to grow up and learn what real power means. It means giving up your freedom, toeing the line, never letting your guard down. Being careful," and she glanced significantly at Laura, then Shiva, "Of those with whom you associate."

"Take us back in time. Go back to before you killed Zokar, please," begged Dom.

"I could," smiled Arlene, "But that would defeat the whole purpose of my little plan, wouldn't it? Shiva would not have anything to be angry about, so he wouldn't keep you two occupied."

Laura turned to stare at Shiva, "This is happening because he is angry?"

"What, did you think I was cooking him? Silly girl. You bring home pets, my dear, you should question their pedigree first. I imagine Shiva was always quite contented with you and Zokar around, eh? Never had any real reason to get upset?"

Laura blinked, "That's not true, I've seen him get really mad once or twice…." But she felt her own voice trail off uncertainly even as she spoke. It was true, Shiva always seemed to have that edge of control in his manner, even when he was yelling at her for something she did.

"Ah, you see?" said Arlene, "You've never seen him really, really lose it, have you?"

"He was always so happy, so nice," said Laura.

"Well, of course, he could just turn on the charm and get anything he wanted, couldn't he?" said Arlene, "Even Zokar succumbed to his charms, and that's saying something."

"Like father, like son. Ataar succumbed to your charms, Mother. What good has that done you now?" growled Dom.

Arlene looked away from them all and said, "Enough! You two have your hands full here. This little monster will keep most of your powers occupied. Take the throne, Laura, and try to be nice to everyone. It wouldn't do for them to all realize that you're both about as dangerous as newborn kittens now, would it? Oh, I'll pop in occasionally and do a few parlour tricks, give you the credit, keep the pundits happy, keep your image up, so to speak. But you will do what I want in the meantime, or there will be hell to pay. Hell in the form of me disabling your little stasis field and letting your erstwhile friend here wake up again."

"Why are you doing this, Mother?" asked Dom.

"It has become exceptionally clear to me over the last twenty-two years, Dom, that your loyalty lies with your twin sister, not with me. And you, Laura. You…" she walked over and gazed at Laura, "These wolves that raised you, these Terrans, for some reason you have given your loyalty to them. I cannot trust either of you, and I require both absolute power, and absolute freedom." Arlene smiled, "This way I will have both."

They both glared at her, and she sighed, "Anyway, I'll leave you with your little problem. Oh, and Laura, tell your Terrans ships to *leave my planets alone!*"

"Wait! Mother! You can't leave us like this!" cried Dom incredulously.

"Oh?" smiled Arlene and turned and walked away, her shoes clacking down the long walkway out of the Great Hall. She levitated the pile of bodies at the door up out of her way, then lowered them again, disappearing.

Laura looked to Dom, "What do we do?"

Dom sighed deeply, "Exactly as she said."

He helped Laura localise the stasis to a small area around Shiva, and the people around them all came back to life at once, except Shiva, who stood inside a shimmering, irregular field of molecular agitation where the molecules of the air outside the stasis field smashed into the stasis field and were suddenly suspended. The air began to glow, a white-hot bubble of immobilised molecules.

Dom commented, "That's dangerous," and moved his hands slightly. Laura watched entranced as the air around Shiva began to swirl, and soon he was only vaguely visible inside a slowly swirling column of charged air, which culminated in an apex from which a constant stream of energy led up to the ceiling.

"Won't that drain him?" asked Laura.

"No, it's not from him. That's the power that you and I would normally have access to, being diverted up around the stasis field and leaking out the top," Dom looked at her worried face, and reassured her, "Nothing can hurt him. Looks like the city will have free power while he's like this, too."

"But for how long? How long must he stay like this?" asked Laura. Then she noticed something odd. Ataar Rizian was slinking out a side door. She called to him, "Ataar, we won't harm you, we know this was all Arlene's doing, not yours."

"It's not you I don't trust. It's Arlene," Ataar replied, hesitating.

"Where are you going?" asked Dom.

"The Core," replied Ataar.

"But why, Ataar?" called Laura.

"I just told you. I don't trust Arlene," replied Ataar and disappeared.

Laura and Dom looked at each other, puzzled, and Laura said, "What? That doesn't make sense."

"Ataar always makes sense," Dom pointed out, looking just as puzzled.

Just then Ataar stuck his head back in the door and called out, "Don't you kids do anything stupid until I get back!"

Trudi suddenly turned to Laura and said, "I'm going with him."

"What?" asked Laura, incredulously.

But Trudi had disappeared.

Dom sat on the floor and sighed, "Well, this sucks. This really sucks."

"That's got to be the understatement of the millennium," sighed Laura and sat beside him staring at Shiva. After a while she commented, "This explains a lot about Shiva though."

"I guess. Arlene seems to know what he is, but I don't think she recognized him at first. I'm sure she didn't."

"Well, he does look a bit different."

Dom laughed, "That's an understatement, too. I always thought it was odd, how neither of us could ever read him. I should have realized he was different."

"I'm glad he's like this," whispered Laura.

"Why?" asked Dom.

"If he's in stasis, he can't miss Zokar."

"I miss Zokar," said Dom quietly.

"You? You hardly knew him!" exclaimed Laura.

Dom stared at her, "He raised me until I was fifteen."

"What?" asked Laura incredulously.

203

"He was my stepbrother, remember? Mum wasn't really... well, she didn't like Zokar, because he was her stepson, and I followed him around a lot as a kid. That really irritated her. He taught me a lot of cool Elvish tricks. He was my big brother, and when I left to look for you he was the one who came with me and helped me run the ship, until the Bug War started and he went back to Atlantis when I was fifteen."

"Wait, he helped you look for me for nine years? He never mentioned that! And he always pretended he didn't know you. Why?"

"Zokar didn't want to be connected to the Royal family. His father married into the line, but Zokar didn't like the Royal lifestyle and he didn't like Arlene."

"I can see why," growled Laura.

"You realize I will kill my mother for what she did to him," stated Dom calmly, and Laura looked into the dark blue eyes, trying to fathom their depths.

"How can you say that? She is our mother."

"Biologically, yes, but as I just told you, Zokar really raised me. He was more family to me than she ever was. I have seen her attitude to you and it has made me angry, but up until now I have forgiven her everything she has done. But this? What possible purpose did killing Zokar serve? He was no threat to the Empire."

"I wish I knew all this before. He was so closed in. The only one who he would ever talk to was Shiva. Even Trudi said that he never spoke to her about his past."

"No, he talked to Ataar too."

"I wonder why Trudi went with Ataar?"

"Maybe that's why. Maybe she just wanted to find out more about him?"

Laura looked thoughtfully out the door that Ataar and Trudi had disappeared through, and shook her head thoughtfully, but kept her own counsel.

Epilogue

Trudi caught up with Ataar a few hundred metres up the main pedestrian thoroughfare, and tugged at his sleeve. He turned to smile contemptuously down at her and said, "So, Terran, you would throw your lot in with me. Is it because I remind you of him?"

"No," replied Trudi grimly.

Ataar stopped and stared down at her, his eyes softening slightly as he saw her burnt fingers. They must be painful, but she did not seem to feel them. Perhaps there was a pain in her heart greater than that of the burns. He looked at her anew. "No?"

She met his gaze levelly, and after a while Ataar said, "You are a clever one, aren't you? Psychic, too, that could come in handy."

"I can't read you," replied Trudi.

"Few can," he said shortly, and they turned and trotted down the thoroughfare together, Trudi keeping up easily with the tall elf.

"What's at the Core?" she asked.

"I'm not sure," said Ataar abruptly.

"Yes you are," countered Trudi.

"Shut up," he snapped.

"Well don't tell me I'm clever then treat me like I'm stupid," she said.

Ataar was stonily silent.

"You're just like him," she sighed.

They trotted on in silence for a while, then the elf muttered, "Thank you."

Trudi asked again, "What's at the Core?"

Ataar smiled dangerously and didn't answer for a moment, then asked, "You seek vengeance, human?"

Trudi nodded.

Ataar's smiled broadened, "Then come with me."

About the Author

Sam Taylor (Author)

Sam Taylor is an Australian science fiction author who has previously written 'Deadly Jewel' to which 'The Eye of Shiva' is the sequel. Sam is also the editor of 'Tales from the Perseus Arm' featuring such authors as John Gribbin and Rachael Kelly (Irish Aspiring Novelist award winner in 2014). Sam's website can be found at www.deadlyjewel.com

Patricia Burn (Cover Artist)

Patricia Burn is the Preferred Artist of SGA Publications, a highly qualified commercial artist and the world's only Consulting Artist. Patricia also does freelance work as well as her work with SGA. Her website can be found at **www.patriciaburn.com**.

Original base cover image: Nasa (Casey Reed)

Other titles by Sam Taylor:

Deadly Jewel (prequel to The Eye of Shiva)
http://www.amazon.com/Deadly-Jewel-Sam-Taylor/dp/0987320211

Tales from the Perseus Arm (edited by Sam Taylor)
with stories by John Gribbin, Sam Taylor, Rachael Kelly and CM Martin
http://www.amazon.com/Tales-Perseus-Arm-Anthologies-ebook/dp/B00EW2WULE

www.sgapublications.com

www.ingramcontent.com/pod-product-compliance
Lightning Source LLC
Chambersburg PA
CBHW060930180626
46817CB00004B/1475